SHIMMER

SHIMMER

DALLAS REED

HARPER TEEN

An Imprint of HarperCollins*Publishers*

HarperTeen is an imprint of HarperCollins Publishers.

Library of Congress Cataloging-in-Publication Data
Reed, Dallas.
Shimmer / Dallas Reed. — 1st ed.
   p.   cm.
Summary: When the opening of a weird box releases a viruslike
ailment that turns the citizens of a remote Colorado town into
deranged and sometimes deadly maniacs, a group of high-school
students flees through a blizzard, struggling to survive.
ISBN 978-0-06-117737-8 (pbk.)
[1. Survival—Fiction. 2. Blizzards—Fiction. 3. Supernatural—
Fiction. 4. Colorado—Fiction. 5. Horror stories.] I. Title.
PZ7.P38413Blo 2009   2008022380
[Fic]—dc22   CIP
                                                            AC

Typography by Joel Tippie
1 2 3 4 5 6 7 8 9 10

First Edition

SHIMMER

They would always remember this coldest December. . . .

The town was called Winter, and it rested in the mountains of Colorado. Over the years, it had endured the harshest of conditions. Situated as it was in a valley walled by towering mountain peaks, Winter found itself isolated when the weather turned snowy and brutal. In such times, the residents stoked fires and ate hearty soups and waited for the skies to clear. They listened to the wind screaming through the valley like an army of wounded ghosts. They watched the snowfall, which could turn from beautiful sprinkles of snowflakes to blinding white blizzard in a matter of minutes. It had been that way since the first settlers had entered the valley and declared the land home.

So when the villainous weather began in mid-December, Winter's people took it in stride.

They couldn't know that something worse than snow and ice—something ancient—was coming for them. It had waited in a mountain cave for aeons, but its time of waiting was over.

This ancient thing had a simple shape.

It was a box.

And what lurked inside wanted out.

The refrigerator was empty, and Emma Driscoll groaned, because it meant she'd have to buy something from one of the vending machines at school. What good was having a chef for a mother if the woman never brought food into the house? Well, Emma didn't have time to worry about it; she was running late for the bus.

Grabbing her black parka with the faux-fur-lined hood, she ran to the door and threw it open in time to see the bus easing toward the corner. "Oh, crap," she muttered, fumbling with the house keys. She managed to lock the door and get her parka on before the bus came to a stop, but she was going to miss her ride if she didn't run. Emma juggled her books, secured them against her chest, and started running.

She hated taking the bus, but she figured she'd hate *missing* the bus more. School was two miles from the duplex her mother rented. It was already snowing and the wind was picking up. There was no way she was walking, so she ran.

But running wasn't easy. Deep snow slowed her steps no matter how hard she willed her legs to move. The bus door began to close though Emma was still two houses away.

"Hey!" she cried. "Wait!"

She poured on the steam. The bus's doors closed, and her heart sank, but she kept running, grateful the vehicle wasn't yet pulling away.

In any other city the school board would have already declared a snow day, but not in Winter. Apparently, snow was so common that half the school year would be forfeited if they let a few inches of accumulation close things down.

"Wait!" she repeated, gasping in a lungful of icy air.

She was out of breath by the time she reached the bus. Normally, she could have run ten times as far and not even broken a sweat, but the freezing cold and the thick snow exhausted her prematurely. She leaned on the side of the bus and knocked on the door with a flat palm.

Oh great, I forgot my gloves, she thought.

The door opened and a wall of welcomed heat poured out. "Thank you," Emma told the bus driver, a heavy man in his late forties whose name she did not know.

6

"Welcome," he said, slapping the doors closed behind her. "Find a seat. I can't move this crate until you're sitting down."

"I'm on it," Emma said, still out of breath. She looked down the aisle of the bus, trying to ignore the glares of disdain she received from three quarters of the kids.

In Winter, Colorado, there was a feud underway. It had been going on for some time now, and it was between the longtime residents of the city and a bunch of newcomers. Though always a retreat for the wealthy, Winter was not a full-blown resort like Vail or Aspen, but that was rapidly changing. Not so long ago, ranching and copper mining were the money games in Winter, but now it was tourism. In the last three years, new condominium complexes and boutique hotels had sprung up in the village along with a number of high-end shops. The new hotel, where Emma's mother would be a chef, was pretty much the nail in the coffin of the old ways. The Hawthorn Resort and Spa was a twenty-two-floor building the color of sandstone. Emma thought the place looked cool, really chic compared to the old lodge-y looking hotels on the edge of the village, but she knew the locals thought it was awful, like a statue built to the gods of progress.

Since her mother was employed by this evil enterprise, naturally the town kids hated her: She was part of the problem, part of the invading force, climbing their mountain to destroy them with iPhones and flat-panel LCD televisions—not that Emma or her mother could afford either of those. As if moving to a new town wasn't hard enough, she'd walked into class that first day feeling like a convict headed to the lethal-injection gurney.

Near the back of the bus, a hand shot up, and Emma was thrilled to see her only friend. She waved back and moved faster down the aisle.

Christina Brown insisted on being called Betina. Betina wore all-black outfits, giving her an overly serious look. As Betina explained it, she was neo-goth. She admired the despondence of the goth movement, but thought the overall look was for crap, so she accentuated her dark attire with simple jewelry and almost no makeup. She also resisted dyeing her hair black, preferring it to remain a natural dirty blond.

Emma walked a little faster over the wet floor where clumps of snow melted into the narrow grooves of the rubber mat. The air in the bus was humid, and it smelled of damp wool and cotton. It was a familiar, even pleasant, scent, Emma thought. Just like in elementary school and middle school. So many other things changed, but not the funky scent of a school bus on a snowy day.

She took the seat next to Betina and noticed that her friend had written *School Blows* in the condensation on the window. She also noticed Betina had excellent penmanship.

"You shouldn't have run," Betina said dryly. "He wasn't going anywhere."

"No reason everyone should have to wait for me."

"That's so not goddess. It's reverse goddess. Antigoddess, if you will."

"You get weirder every day."

"I'm a calendar of the bizarre."

Emma laughed and leaned back in the seat. "I figure most of these kids hate me enough without adding to the problem by holding up the bus."

"They'd hate you, anyway."

"Thanks, Betina."

"Look, it's tribal. They had something and now other people are coming in to take it away from them, and most of them are too stupid to realize it wasn't all that great to begin with."

"So they hate what I represent?"

"No," Betina said. "I'm pretty sure it's you."

Emma laughed again and slapped her friend's shoulder. "Did you get your assignment done for Dickinson's class?"

Betina pulled a notebook out of her black bag and opened it. She searched its contents for a moment and yanked out three sheets of paper that had been stapled together. Across the top of the front page, printed in eighteen-point bold font, were the words: *Written Under Duress.*

"You didn't."

"What choice did I have?" Betina asked. "An end-of-semester book report? Come on. How lame. It was obviously Dickinson's attempt to manipulate our time with irrelevant busywork. The reading list had nothing to do with our course of study. It's a blatant power play that I for one will not let pass unnoted."

"He's so going to fail you."

"He can't fail me. I did the work. It's how you change the system from within."

Emma had worked really hard on her report, both its content and its presentation, but she liked Mr. Dickinson and loved his class, so she didn't see the report as a burden. It was hard, but only because she wanted it to be good. Her mother always told her that grades were the only asset she would have when she applied to colleges. They'd never had much money, and certainly not enough to fund Emma's higher education, so she needed to keep the grades up and apply for every academic scholarship she could find. That meant playing by the rules.

Betina's parents had probably put more than enough away for their daughter to attend whatever college she wanted. Knowing Betina, though, she was more the type to bum around for a year or two before settling into anything as "normal" as college. She might not even *want* to go.

"So what are we going to do during the break?" Betina asked. "I so can't bear the idea of spending two weeks with my family."

"I don't know," Emma replied, feeling a flash of relief. She'd worried that since she was new, she wouldn't have anyone to hang out with over the holiday break. The Hawthorn Resort was opening on Christmas Eve, so her mother would be working long hours, and their duplex wasn't really close to anything. She was grateful to know that Betina was staying in town, though she had no idea what they'd do. "What do you usually do around here? I'm new, remember?"

"We do nothing," Betina said blandly. "We are nothing. We watch the snow fall and then watch the snow melt. This year, we'll watch ten thousand tourists descend on us, and we'll laugh at their false joy, knowing happiness is merely a rest stop on the long, hellish road of life. Sound like fun?"

"Totally."

They both laughed, completely oblivious to the other kids around them. Finally Betina resumed her sullen expression and stared out the window. "We'll figure something out," she said, poking the glass with her finger. "But nothing really happens around here."

2

Justin Moore paused in the hallway and peered into his dad's home office. He wasn't snooping, because the door was wide open. Besides, he didn't really care what his pops kept in the room. Still, he paused, because there was a strange box sitting on the desk. It was small, like if you made a cube out of CD cases, and it seemed to be carved from some deep gray stone. *Weird*, he thought.

Ahead in the kitchen, his stepmother called for him to hurry up: "Breakfast is getting cold."

Justin left the doorway and continued on to the kitchen, where he found his stepmother, Brandy, leaning over the stove. Justin liked Brandy well enough. She was cool, if a little out there. Today she wore her lavender running suit and her matching running shoes. *It must be Thursday*, he thought. *Pilates.*

Whatever she was cooking smelled awful, but then it usually did. Brandy always "experimented" with food, like a mad scientist with a Cuisinart. She spent hours watching cooking shows, taking notes, and nodding her head as if those bozo chefs were speaking directly to her, but she somehow never quite got the hang of fixing a meal that could slip easily past his gag reflex.

Just once he'd like to come into the kitchen and discover bacon and scrambled eggs that hadn't undergone one of Brandy's insane experiments. Hell, he'd be happy enough with cold cereal or Pop-Tarts. He supposed it was cool she tried; he just wished she'd find another guinea pig.

"Hey," Justin said.

"Morning, honey," Brandy replied. "Breakfast is on the table."

Justin passed through the kitchen to the dining table, where his baby brother was already strapped into a high chair. Brendan was ten months old, and Justin loved the little guy.

"How's the rock star?" Justin asked of Brendan.

"Goo-aw," Brendan said.

"That's right, keep it real." Justin leaned over and kissed the top of his kid brother's head, then looked down at the table, where he was greeted by a plate of . . . well . . . he really didn't know.

"It's huevos rancheros," Brandy called cheerfully from the kitchen. "Italian style."

Not knowing exactly what to make of the description, Justin thanked his stepmother and sat next to his brother.

"Goo-aw."

"I couldn't agree more," Justin said in an imitation of his father's voice.

"Goo-AW!"

Justin laughed and turned to the nightmare on his plate. He knew eggs were somehow involved in the Technicolor sewage, though their exact whereabouts eluded him. A thick red paste flecked with green and brown covered a substantial lump at the plate's center. Chunks of sausage, bright pink against the crimson sauce, stuck out like bits of lung from a gaping chest wound.

Nice imagery, he thought. As if it wasn't going to be hard enough to eat without that nod to slasher flicks.

Brandy strolled in with her own breakfast: two pieces of dry toast and a mug of coffee.

"Now, your father and I will be gone when you get home from school," Brandy reminded him.

"Yep," Justin said. "And the orgy will start promptly at six."

"Well, you play safe," Brandy said.

"You didn't think I was serious?"

Brandy shrugged and took a bite of toast.

She *had* thought he was serious. Justin shook his head and returned his attention to the mess on his plate. He cut a forkful of the solid substance loose and jabbed it with the fork. He took a bite and felt his cheeks flush. Nasty.

"Look, I know your father has his rule about parties," Brandy continued, "but it might be a good way to make some friends. I still feel really bad that we dragged you out here away from your friends in Houston, so I left a little something for you in the microwave. If you decide to have a few kids over, you can at least have something to eat."

Justin was afraid to ask what Brandy might have left in the microwave. He knew damn well the last thing he would do if anyone actually came over was feed them something of her creation. Poisoning didn't exactly make a guy Mr. Popularity.

"Thank you," he said, nearly choking. What the hell was in this stuff?

"Not with your mouth full, honey."

Justin nodded. Next to him, Brendan was gurgling and slapping at the tray of his high chair, seeming as happy as could be.

"Are you sure you don't want to come along,

Justin?" Brandy looked too serious and a bit pouty—always big with the drama.

"It's your second honeymoon," he said. "Besides, you've got the rock star to take care of. I'll be skiing the whole time. Don't sweat it."

"Well, try to make some friends."

His dad wandered into the kitchen. He was a burly man with thick dark hair brushed straight back. His face was round, and if he'd had a neck, Justin had never seen it. This morning he wore a blue sport shirt and black slacks, looking like an extra from *The Sopranos*.

Brandy turned and looked over her shoulder. "Let me get you something," she called.

"Don't bother," Jim Moore replied.

"Suit yourself, but I made huevos rancheros, Italian style."

"Yeah well, I'm sure I can get diarrhea in New York."

Brandy turned back to Justin and said, "Tell him how good it is."

He'd managed only three bites the whole time he'd been sitting at the dining table, but he figured he shouldn't have to suffer alone. "Yeah, Dad. They're pretty damn good."

"Really?" his dad asked, leaning back to peer into the dining room. He looked hopeful for a moment, then must have seen through the lie on Justin's smiling face. "Yeah," he said. "I'll just grab something at the hotel."

"You're missing out," Brandy said.

"Eh. Oh, hey! Justin." Jim Moore hurried into the dining room and crossed to the far side of the table to face him. "I got this thing in my office. Someone is going to come by tomorrow to pick it up." Jim pointed his finger at Justin and wagged it as he spoke. "Now, I don't want you mucking around with it. Just leave it on my desk until the guy gets here. He's some professor from D.U."

"Is it that box thing?"

His dad scowled. "You been in my office?"

"No," Justin said. "Your door was open. I saw it when I was coming down the hall."

Looking suspicious, yet convinced, his dad nodded. "Yeah, that's it."

"What is it?"

"Don't know. The blast crew found it Tuesday night. It was in a cave near the peak. They opened up a whole maze of the damned things blasting that snow away. Anyhow, they brought it down, and it looked strange enough to be worth something. Teddy eyeballed it and thought we should have an expert give it a look. He emailed a few shots of the thing to this professor he knows, and now the guy wants to come out and give it a closer look."

"I have school tomorrow, you know."

"I'm fully aware of your schedule, sport. He'll be here around four. Just give him the box and be done with it. Now, do you have everything you need before we go?"

"I got the plastic."

"Good. And what is my rule about parties?"

Justin sat up straight and crossed his hands in his lap, then somberly said, "If I have a party, it will serve as my funeral and my wake."

"I'm serious."

"No kidding," Justin said. He stood up and rubbed the top of Brendan's head.

"Goo-wa-wa-phft."

"He's serious," Justin whispered, watching his dad's cheeks turn red. "Thanks for the grub, Brandy. I got to get my groovy on."

"You're welcome, honey," Brandy said, apparently not noticing that he hadn't eaten even half of the meal.

Justin walked down the hall to his bedroom. Inside he crossed to the printer and lifted the stack of pages from its rack. He read the headline and nodded, thinking it looked good enough.

It read:

AVALANCHE PARTY!

3

Russ Foster heard the front door click closed and opened his eyes. He gazed at the ceiling, wiped the sleep away, and rolled over to see what his alarm clock had to say. A flash of fear ran through his chest as he read the digital display, but he couldn't focus yet. At first, it looked like he'd slept two extra hours, but that number wasn't a nine; it was a seven. He wasn't late for school.

"Coffee," he groaned, rolling out of bed. "Much coffee."

He trudged bleary-eyed across his bedroom, stepping on discarded clothes and nearly kicking his snowboard before making it to the safety of the hallway. The house was chilly, and he rubbed his arms to smooth out the goose bumps. He scratched his head, sending tingles down the back of his neck. In the kitchen he found the pot of coffee, still half full.

"Thanks, Dad," he muttered.

He poured a cup and carried it back to his bedroom, where he sat on the edge of the bed. The snowboard caught his eye, and Russ cast a glance over his shoulder at the window to see a line of snow accumulated on a tree branch. It occurred to him that today would be an excellent day to reject public education and thrash some powder.

The board was a white Burton Custom X. It was sick. He loved the thing, and he'd never imagined owning one. No way Russ or his dad, Red Foster, could afford that sweet board, but some rich tourist had left it behind last season, probably fed up with eating ice and bruising ass. Red had claimed it from the lost and found at the lodge and presented it to his son. Russ had about fallen over with gratitude. Then he'd hit the peak every day for a week with his buddy Kit Urban.

Russ's dad didn't make a lot of money running the plows and the tram system for the city, but he did get free lift passes and the occasional shopping spree at the lodge's lost and found. Hopefully he'd have the same privileges once the new hotel opened. There weren't a lot of benefits to living in a mountain town, but the few Russ could think of—free boarding, a seasonal parade of tourist girls, and frequent snow days—pretty much rocked.

Today wasn't a snow day, though, and Russ sipped his

coffee, struggling with the thought of leaving his board behind and spending all day at McKinley High. The winter break was only a couple days off, he reasoned. Only two more days in the stuffy, overheated halls of education before two weeks of nothing. He could survive it. He didn't want to, but one of the few rules Red Foster imposed on Russ was "Keep your ass in school," and since Red was cool about so many other things, Russ did his best to accommodate the request.

"Not today, buddy," Russ told the board.

He stood from the edge of the bed and carried his coffee with him to the bathroom. He shaved and showered quickly. Once dressed, he grabbed his backpack and returned to the kitchen for more coffee while he waited for Kit to show up.

Russ and Kit had been friends since grade school. They boarded together, played video games, and spent weekend evenings in the village catching movies, drinking coffee, and hanging out. Kit had white-blond hair that hung in his eyes. He wore baggy shorts and T-shirts nearly year round, regardless of weather, because Kit was convinced he had the soul of a surfer and only his unfortunate residence a couple thousand miles from any viable beach kept him from being a major player on the surfing circuit. Russ thought it was pretty funny. Kit could barely manage his board on a slope, and that wasn't rising and falling all around him like waves would.

Russ sat in Kit's car with oven-hot air blowing over his face from the dash vents. They cruised around the edge of the village toward school. As usual, Kit was convinced the world was plotting against him.

". . . and then our property taxes are going to skyrocket, right? So it's like we won't even be able to afford our houses, even if we already own them. And it's not like we can just sell them, because we still couldn't afford another house in town. That's how they drive us out, right? That's how they take over."

"It's not an alien invasion," Russ said with a laugh.

"Might as well be," Kit countered. "The Monies come to town, and all the locals either fight or submit. It's a total sci-fi scenario, except what divides us are financial classes, not solar systems."

"Whatever," Russ said, shaking his head.

He knew Kit was basically right, but he didn't see the point in getting worked up over the whole thing. It wasn't like Russ intended to lie down in front of bulldozers or torch anyone's house in protest. His dad always said, "You can't fight progress," and Russ knew his old man was right. The Monies had already landed; they'd already conquered the world. It had just taken them a while to find Winter on the map.

"'*Whatever*'?" Kit said. "Dude, that is the battle cry of the überlame."

"Look, we graduate next year. After that, we can go wherever the hell we want."

"That's like seeing a lesion on the back of your hand and saying, 'Oh, it's just skin cancer. I won't look at it anymore.' It spreads, man. It spreads."

"What?" Russ said through a splutter of laughter. "Turn the drama down, Kit."

"You wait. They are going to run all of us out of town."

"They can't. They need people to cook their meals and clean their streets. They need people to fix their cars and paint their houses."

"Weak, dude. I wasn't born to serve, especially not *them*. We're not lower rungs on the food chain, right? But Capitalism is this socially endorsed hyper-evolution: The strong survive, and the rest of us get eaten."

"Not much you can do about it."

"I refuse to submit to the inevitable."

"The word for that is 'crazy.' Besides, it's not all bad."

"Yeah?" Kit asked. "Name one good thing the Monies bring with them."

"Females," Russ said, smiling.

"True dat," Kit said excitedly. "Damn, there have been some babes crawling the halls this year. It's like a Wal-Mart of hotness. . . ."

Thank god, Russ thought. Another trait Kit possessed was the attention span of a gerbil on crack. Most times his conspiratorial rants could be defused with the right key word or phrase. Girls usually did the trick.

These days when Russ thought about girls, he couldn't help but think about Emma Driscoll. She was a girl in his calculus class who sat next to Betina Brown. Ever since he first saw her, she'd been on Russ's mind. Her mother was going to be a cook or something with the new resort. Russ knew because he'd asked a couple kids at school, though he'd never worked up the courage to speak with Emma directly. Strange thing. Girls didn't usually throw his cool into shock, but Emma damn sure did. What was that all about? Maybe it was because she didn't seem as clueless as most of the girls Russ had grown up with, and she didn't have the attitude most of the new girls brought with them. She wasn't a Money, but something about her just shut his mind down.

Next to him, Kit kept up the dialogue.

". . . it's like a fairy godmother waved a wand over all the uggos and they turned into princesses. Totally magic."

Russ laughed. Kit was right. Beautiful girls were like magic. The only magic Russ had ever seen, anyway.

4

Emma looked through the windows of the bus, thinking the village of Winter looked absolutely beautiful under its frosting of white. On her left, the ridge that separated the town from the resort area jutted skyward wearing a smooth coat of snow. The school bus rolled on at a slow pace. Though the roads had been recently plowed, patches of ice marked the streets, and the bus driver was cautious. Next to her, Betina slumped with her feet on the seat ahead, wedging herself in as she picked at a thread on her scarf.

As they climbed down from the bus, the freezing air slapped Emma's cheeks. She was shivering uncontrollably by the time they walked through the front doors of the school.

Standing in the middle of the wet linoleum floor was a boy with tangles of dark brown hair. He was tall and slender with high cheekbones, green eyes, and a killer smile of insanely white teeth. He held a stack of yellow paper and was pulling off sheets, handing them out to everyone who passed him.

"What fresh hell is this?" Betina whispered.

They couldn't help but pass the boy on the way to their lockers, though Betina refused to look at him as they walked by. Emma did look, not only because she was curious about what his flyers said, but also because he was a hottie.

He didn't have the TV-star pretty-boy look, not exactly. He was that kind of hot, only it looked natural on him, not like stylists had spent an hour on his hair and outfit.

Emma reached out for one of the flyers, and the boy yanked it away. She stopped, shocked by the rebuke. She felt her cheeks turn bright red and started walking again, hoping to get far away from the boy before he saw how embarrassed she was.

"Hey," he said. "Wait."

Emma paused and looked at him again, thinking now would be a good time to apply some of the attitude Betina was so fond of throwing around.

The boy beamed at her. "Sorry about that," he said. "I mean, it's a party invite."

"And every other random kid is invited but me?"

"No," he said. "God, no. I just wanted to invite you personally."

"Oh," Emma said, blushing now for a different reason. She looked around for Betina, who was gazing at the ceiling as if she'd never been so inconvenienced in her life.

"My name's Justin," he said. "And you are personally invited."

Then he handed her a flyer with the headline AVALANCHE PARTY!

"Promise me you'll be there."

She read over the page quickly. "Tonight?"

"Yep."

"I don't know."

"You have to be there," Justin said. "It's a social imperative."

"I'll try," Emma told him, now feeling way uncomfortable with excitement.

"Promise."

"I'll try," she repeated, then hurried away to join Betina.

"What is it?" her friend asked.

"It's a party. Tonight. Do you think we should go?"

Betina sighed and took the flyer from Emma. She read over the page as they walked into the corridor where their lockers lined the walls.

"Well?" Emma asked. "Do you want to go?"

Betina handed the flyer back to her and said, "It may be the only thing I have left to live for."

5

Justin hooked his iPod into the house's sound system and cued up the party mix he'd thrown together. He did a quick survey of the place, walking first through the living room and dining room, which were really just two large parts of a mammoth open-floor plan. He liked the house. It had high ceilings with exposed beams running through the air, and the wall facing the mountain peak was all glass. He could have lived without the elk head over the fireplace—so not cool—and the mirror in the dining room, which was framed with hundreds of tiny antlers laid one over the other in a herringbone pattern, but for the most part, the place was wide open and the view of the mountain was kicking.

In the kitchen his gaze fell on the microwave, and he groaned. He was afraid to open the door, dreading whatever abomination Brandy had left there. He decided it was better to get it over with before any guests arrived and opened the door.

On the glass tray sat a stack of twenty-dollar bills

with a note attached.

"Nice," he said, reaching in and retrieving the money. Quickly counting it on the tiled countertop, he discovered Brandy had left him three hundred bucks with which to *Have some fun*, or so the note said. "Nice," he repeated, grinning.

Though his father made a buttload of cash developing properties all around the country, he was a stingy old bastard. He gave Justin a credit card, not because he believed his son should have financial freedom, but because he wanted to know about every cent Justin spent. He had a five-hundred-dollar monthly limit, and if he exceeded it, Pops took the plastic away for two weeks.

"That's what happens when you don't manage your money," Jim Moore had always said. "You end up with nothing."

Justin had barely scraped enough together to buy a keg of beer for the party, and snacks would have been limited to the bags of chips Brandy kept in the back of the pantry. But with her generous contribution to his party fund, he could order pizzas for everybody and still have some left over for the weekend.

All day he'd handed out his flyers, and he'd met a lot of girls doing it. He might just find himself with a date this weekend, and some extra cash couldn't hurt.

He wasn't worried about people showing up. They were already discussing it in the school's chat room. Of course, the popular kids were all "Maybe, if nothing good's on the tube," but there were some solid yeses in the crowd. Besides, it didn't really matter how many showed up or how popular they were; Justin liked throwing parties, and he had a history of being grounded to prove it.

That was one of the reasons he'd planned the party for a school night. His pops would probably have one of the workmen swing by to check on the place Friday and Saturday night, because Jim Moore was a control freak with a capital FREAK. That wasn't as likely to happen on a Thursday.

He checked the freezer for ice and decided there would be enough. On the far end of the counter he looked over the four large bowls of chips.

"Check," he said. "Time to secure the premises."

He crossed the house and walked into his bedroom, where he retrieved a stack of signs he'd printed up. They all said: DO NOT ENTER, but each one had a little funny note below. Things like:

Beware of Sheep

Don't Make Me Get Medieval on Your Ass

And . . .

All Beer Privileges Revoked upon Entry

Justin started at the door of his parents' bedroom and walked through the house taping the signs to rooms he didn't want trashed. He returned to the home office and did a walk-through to make sure no important papers were sitting around. It wasn't likely. His pops kept the place neat. But if some folder full of bank statements or spread sheets or whatever kinds of paperwork his dad collected got beer spilled on it, Justin would be toastier than Joan of Arc. Yeah, he had the signs, but those didn't always work. In fact, some kids took the off-limits thing as a challenge.

Finding no documentation lying around, Justin's attention fell on the small stone box atop his pops's desk. Justin dropped into the chair and slid close to give the thing a look.

It was a dark gray color and the sides were rough and uneven. What he hadn't noticed from the hall that morning was the rusted metal band that circled the box two thirds of the way up. It seemed to have a locking mechanism of some sort, which looked pretty cool—a kind of metal thorn jutting out above an angled hole in the middle of the faceplate. Justin touched the sides of the box with his palms and quickly pulled them away.

"Gross," he muttered, leaning back.

The box didn't feel like stone at all. If anything, it felt like doughy skin. Justin leaned forward to get a better look at the thing.

What the hell? he wondered. He reached out a finger and touched the rusted plate of metal, grateful to discover it was simply that: metal. He ran his finger off of the faceplate and drew it along the odd, spongy surface of the box. The texture was more than weird; it creeped him out bad.

Better hide this thing, he thought. *It could be a rare artifact or something. Pops would blow a gasket if anything happened to it.*

Justin stood and lifted the box by gently pushing the sides of his hands against the metal band. He looked around the office for a functional hiding place. His dad kept the drawers of his desk and filing cabinets locked—even locked the closet door, which had been fitted with a dead bolt after they'd moved in. Justin settled for putting the box on the floor, far back beneath his dad's desk. Someone would have to work

pretty hard to find the thing, and it would be pro-
tected from accidental brew spills.

"Done," he said.

Now he'd wait for the guests to arrive.

6

Russ stood in the corner of Justin's living room and observed the party with a long sweeping glance. It was just like school, he thought. Well, it was just like school with beer, free pizza, and loud music. The Cools all gathered by the windows across the room, surrounding their queen, Tess Ward, and hanging on her every dumbass word. The Sweats—those jocks who weren't cool enough to be Cool—hung next to the popular group by the window. The Geek faction stood by the fireplace, their attention drawn to the computer-managed entertainment system. On the humongous flat-panel television screen behind them, an episode of *Family Guy* played on mute while Fall Out Boy roared over the speakers. Though the groups were segregated now, Russ knew the interaction between them would increase exponentially with the amount of beer consumed. But for now, it was like school: a place for every clique and every clique in its place. He drained his cup of beer and leaned back on the wall.

"Slammin'," Kit said. "Epic party."

"I thought you hated the Monies," Russ said.

"I make exceptions for free beer."

"Well, don't get too used to it. Once he settles into the Cools, I'm guessing his parties will be Evite only, and we probably won't be on the list."

"That sucks," Kit said, losing his smile. "How do you know he's going to land with the Cools?"

"Look around," Russ told him. "This place is so Tess-friendly, I'm surprised she hasn't already announced their engagement. Besides, she's been scoping him all night. Every time he gets close to the Cools, she acts like she doesn't see him. Total mating dance. Check it out." Russ lifted his chin to indicate the crowd across the room.

As if on cue, Justin Moore approached the crowd by the window. He was holding a pitcher of beer and offering to fill cups. Tess Ward turned away—so obvious—and looked out the window, pretending to take in the view of the night-shrouded mountains.

Kit started laughing uncontrollably. He held a hand over his face and shook his head.

"She might as well wear a sign that says 'Do me.'" Russ turned away from Tess and her crowd. He was looking for someone else.

In first-period calculus, he'd overheard Emma talking with Betina. She was supposed to be at Justin's party. At least, that's what she'd said.

He didn't see her when he scoped the living room. He looked at his beer cup. Its emptiness made a good enough excuse to wander. Maybe Emma Driscoll had slipped in and was hanging in the kitchen or in one of the bedrooms.

"Come on," he said, slapping Kit lightly on the shoulder, "I'm empty."

"Hold on. Hold on," Kit said excitedly. "Tess is making her move."

And Kit was right. Russ looked up in time to see Tess turning away from the window and holding out her cup. The rich boy, Justin, said something to her while he topped off her drink, and Tess threw back her head and laughed. She flipped a ribbon of perfect blond hair over her shoulder and reached out with her hand to touch Justin's arm.

"The unwary prey is now trapped," Kit said dramatically, like the host of an Animal Planet special. "It is only a matter of time now before the sad and inevitable outcome."

"I don't see him complaining," Russ said. "Come

on. My cup isn't filling itself, and it looks like our beer wench is being detained."

He wanted to get away from this scene. He wanted to find Emma.

7

Justin thought the party was kicking ass. Everyone had food and drink, and the tunes were banging. Even the Cools had thawed out and spoken to him. Tess Ward had lit up like a Christmas tree when he'd made a lame joke. But now, he couldn't get rid of her. Usually, if a girl that hot was interested, Justin did his best to keep her interested, but there was something about Tess, something that went beyond the typical popular-girl ice princess act. Cruelty seemed to be as natural to her as blue eyes and blond hair. Her edge wasn't appealing; it just cut. After filling her cup and chatting for a few minutes, Justin had walked away to speak with his other guests, but Tess followed him, babbling on and on.

". . . because they look up to me, you know," Tess said. "I'm popular because they need me to be popular. They need someone to envy and to follow. Most sheep do, right?"

"Sure," Justin said. He kept the smile plastered on his face, but he felt anything but pleased.

From the corner of his eye, Justin saw a pack of teens enter the hallway off the living room. His pops's office was down that way, and he paused, ignoring Tess's latest comment so he could make sure the three boys were just headed to the bathroom and not the forbidden territory. Unfortunately, the guys were drunk and they headed straight for the office.

"Crap," Justin said. "Back in a minute."

He hurried across the living room, keeping his eye on the three boys who were already filing into the office. "Hey," he called, but the music was too loud or they were too wasted. Either way, they continued into the room and closed the door.

A moment later, Justin threw open the door and was shocked to see they'd already found the box he'd been so careful to hide. Two boys—typical Jocks with their letterman jackets over cable-knit sweaters— stood by the desk. One had a joint in his mouth, and the other was laughing hysterically. The third was on his knees under the desk and he was holding the box.

"What the hell?" Justin said.

"Just looking for a little privacy to spark a spliff," the boy with the joint said. "You're cool to join us."

"Thanks," Justin replied. "But I meant, what is he doing?"

43

"Laurent dropped the lighter," joint boy said. He shrugged. "It's cool. He'll find it."

"Dude, what the hell is this thing?" Laurent asked from his place on the floor. "It's like a box made of skin or some crap."

"Put it back," Justin said, eyeing the box nervously. The last thing he needed was for one of these wasted guys to fall on the thing and destroy it. "Look, you can light up in my room. It's two doors down. Just open a window."

"Yeah, but what the hell is this thing?" Laurent said. "Doug, Barry, check this thing out."

"Hey!" Justin barked. He crossed the room in two quick steps and took the box from Laurent's hands. "You guys shouldn't be in here, okay? I don't mean to be a dick or anything, but you have to bail. Like I said, my room is two doors down. You can burn that place to the ground, but this room is off-limits."

Joint boy, Doug, nodded his head slowly. "It's cool," he muttered. "It's cool. Just chill. Laurent, you got the fire?"

"Got it." He held up a silver Zippo and waved it in the air.

"Then let's get our exit on."

Doug led Laurent and Barry past Justin and back

into the hall. Justin watched as the three found their way to his room and disappeared inside. When he turned toward the living room, he found Tess Ward standing in the hall.

"What's that?" she asked, pointing at the box.

Justin opened his mouth to reply, but a strange sensation startled him. It felt like the box moved. Not like it had something inside it, but the surface of the box expanded like it was taking in a breath, like it was alive. He nearly dropped the thing.

"It's weird-looking," Tess said.

"Yeah," Justin agreed. "It's weird."

Tess reached out and stroked the top of the box, her fingers grazing its surface. She traced an edge with her index finger, slowly and sensually. "What's it made of?"

"I don't know." Justin walked into the office, away from Tess. "It's my dad's. He'll kill me if anything happens to it."

"We could always stay in here and stand guard," Tess said.

Justin paused and looked at the girl. She gazed back at him through her eyelashes. Her full lips shimmered wetly. Tess stepped into the room and closed the door behind her.

"You were cool to invite everyone," she said, crossing the room to stand only inches away from Justin. "But I've had enough of the loser circus for one night. I like it in here. It's quiet." She smiled, but the expression struck Justin as cold and soulless as the smile of a lizard. "It's private."

Uneasy, Justin backed up a step and felt the edge of his father's desk on his leg. Carefully, he turned and set the box on it, buying himself another couple of seconds to think. He didn't want to be alone with Tess. She was gorgeous and popular, but she creeped him out.

"Maybe we could come back later," he suggested. "I can't leave the circus unattended. Like you said, the sheep need someone to follow. Besides, it's early."

Tess snaked out her arms and wrapped them around his neck. His skin shriveled at her touch. He looked into her clear blue eyes and saw eagerness there. When she kissed him, a finger of ice traced down his spine. The lips carried no warmth or emotion. They were just flesh—like kissing the dead.

Justin pulled away. Tess looked at him the way she would if she'd just given him some priceless gift. She was poised to accept his undying gratitude and adulation, but she didn't get it.

"We'll definitely come back later," he lied. He put his arm around Tess and guided her out of the office.

"Are you blowing me off?" Tess asked. She made it sound like he'd done something impossible, horrible, unbelievable. "My God, do you really think you're that hot?"

"Not hot at all," Justin said. "It's just rude to ignore all of my guests."

"Screw your guests," Tess hissed. She spun on him, fast as a cat. Her palm slapped down on his chest and she pushed him to the wall. "Look, Justin, you'd better understand that zeros will get you nowhere at McKinley, and that room is full of zeros. It doesn't matter how many of them are your friends. Zero times ten is zero. Okay? Now maybe you're a little shy, and that's sexy cool, but if you are blowing me off, you are so going to regret it."

That's enough, Justin thought. He knew the whole high school royalty scenario, and he knew that usually the most admired teens were also the most hated. He didn't need to belong to Tess's clique to survive McKinley High. He didn't need her or her friends at all.

"I can live with regret," he said, and slid out from

under Tess's hand. "Can you live with rejection?"

Justin didn't bother waiting for a response. He walked down the hall back to the living room and rejoined the party.

8

Emma stood with Betina in the kitchen. Instead of beer, Emma was drinking a Diet Coke. The pizza on the counter looked good, but she didn't take a slice. She'd eaten dinner at Betina's house only an hour ago and wasn't hungry. But if she'd known Justin was serving pizza, she would have waited. Betina's parents were vegan, and the dinner—consisting of puréed vegetables, hard bread, and a strange strawberry paste dessert—was kind of gross.

Sipping a Diet Coke of her own, Betina said, "Twenty-three."

"What?"

"Twenty-three," Betina repeated. "That's how many useless kitchen gadgets I've counted since we came in here."

Emma smiled and glanced around the kitchen. She wasn't sure exactly what qualified as a "useless" kitchen gadget, but she noticed several high-tech machines occupying the counters and a shelf above the sink.

"Maybe Justin's mom is a chef like mine."

"Maybe they're gadget hogs who buy everything whether they need it or not."

Emma was going to reply, but suddenly a boy from her calculus class appeared over Betina's shoulder. Emma knew the boy's name was Russ Foster. The first time she had seen him in class, a spark of attraction had flared in her chest, but Russ hadn't so much as said hello to her in the halls. He looked a little older than other boys. There was a maturity there and it weighed heavily in his deep brown eyes. His skin was dark, and his hair was short and messy in exactly the right way. He looked a little rough around the edges, like a thoughtful musician, but he could have just as well been the son of a local rancher. He had a toughness about him. Usually Emma could fit the kids from school into easy categories—a Jock, a Brain, a Burner, a Cool—but Russ eluded such simple classification, which was probably why he continued to intrigue her.

Justin, on the other hand, was easy to classify. He was a hottie from a wealthy family. He was cool and seemed like he had a major sense of humor. Emma had been excited about coming to the party because of him. After his invitation in the school lobby, she'd had some totally outrageous thoughts about the boy. About them dating. About a future. So lame and premature. More than likely he was just a player and he chatted up all the girls the same way.

Betina noticed Emma's distraction and threw a look over her shoulder. When she turned back to Emma, she rolled her eyes. Emma knew her friend wanted to make a smart-ass comment about Russ, but he was too close for her to say anything in secrecy.

Then Russ did a completely surprising thing. He stopped in the middle of the kitchen, turned to Emma, and said, "Hey."

Emma was taken off guard. She managed to say, "Hi."

"We have calculus together," Russ said.

"I know," Emma replied. "You sit behind us."

Nice way to state the obvious, she thought. *All you need to do now is giggle a lot and maybe drool. Then he'll think you're cool.*

"Yeah, right," Russ said.

A silence followed, and Emma didn't know what to do. She knew she was smiling, but did it look stupid? Was it a good yearbook picture smile or was it something tragic like the way you smile when you've done something totally clumsy? The more she thought about it, the stranger the smile felt on her face.

"Hey, Betina," Russ said.

"Hellooooo," Betina said, drawing out the word, sounding annoyed.

Kit Urban joined them in the middle of the kitchen. Emma thought he looked like a surfer—a really strange and totally wired surfer. Why would anyone wear white shorts and a watermelon-colored tank top in the middle of winter? He must have been freezing.

"Great party," he said. "Epic, right?"

"It's nice," Emma said. "Justin's got a beautiful house."

"Yes," Betina said. "We were just trying to figure out where Emma's things would go after the wedding."

"Betina," Emma gasped, feeling a needle of embarrassment work through her ribs.

Russ sneered at the joke and looked away toward the dining room.

"You two hooking up?" Kit asked excitedly.

"I don't even know him," Emma replied quickly, her cheeks burning even more. "I just said he has a nice house."

"You know what people like him are doing to the world, don't you?" Kit asked.

"Systematically destroying the middle class while simultaneously homogenizing the retail experience?" Betina offered.

"Totally!" Kit said. He took a step closer to Betina. She looked aggravated and took a step away.

Emma felt like she should defend Justin. After all, he shouldn't be blamed for his father's occupation, but she didn't get the chance to say anything. The music in the living room died mid-song. The sudden silence felt ominous.

"Thank god," Betina said with a sigh. "One more Emo track and I'd—"

"Put that down!"

Emma recognized the voice as Justin's. He was shouting at someone in the living room, and he sounded really angry.

"Drama!" Betina said, her eyes lighting up with excitement.

Emma, Betina, Russ, and Kit raced from the kitchen to see what was going on. The commotion from the living room grew.

"Put it down," Justin shouted. "And then get the hell out of my house."

Emma was halfway down the length of the dining room when she saw Justin. He faced Tess Ward, who stood in front of the fireplace, holding a box in her hand. Two jocks in letterman jackets, Doug Nichols and Barry Lebbon, held Justin's arms. They were laughing as a third jock stood next to Tess, ready to tackle Justin if he got away. Emma walked closer. She felt Betina and the boys at her back. Standing there, she couldn't help but notice the number of her classmates who had attended the party.

Most people had backed away from the confrontation, though. They muttered and whispered. Some looked excited the way Betina had, the anticipation of violence lighting their faces. Others looked worried, but none of them were doing anything. Why weren't they doing anything?

"What's going on?" Russ asked.

"I'm not sure," Emma told him.

"What is Tess holding?" Kit asked.

"Some kind of box," Emma whispered.

Emma looked at the thing and felt a chill at her neck. Though uniform in shape, the box struck her as somehow unnatural.

"Now," Tess said teasingly, "tell me again what this box does?"

She held the strange gray box out to Justin, taunting him with it, then pulled it close to her chest. Tess petted the top of the box and smiled.

"It doesn't do anything," Justin said. "It's just a box. It's my father's."

"And will Daddy be grumpy if Justy-wusty opens his box?" Tess asked in a mocking baby-talk tone.

Justin struggled against the two boys holding him. He lunged forward but was yanked back before he could tear away. Kids in the crowd gasped. Some laughed.

"Probably a family heirloom," Russ said over Emma's shoulder.

"Why is she doing this?"

"Because she's Tess," Betina said.

Emma felt a sick sensation in her belly. Obviously the box was valuable, or at least had sentimental value to Justin and his family. Tess was treating it like a cheap rubber ball, bouncing it in her hand with absolutely no concern. What if she dropped it? Broke it? It was a level of meanness Emma didn't understand. It wasn't like Tess needed more toys. From everything Emma had heard, Tess's family still owned a third of the valley. Her father was a hotshot land baron or something. She had everything. So why was she so miserable that she had to make everyone around her miserable? Emma just didn't get it.

"Should we revisit our discussion about regret?" Tess asked.

"Leave it alone," Justin said.

Tess turned the box in her hands. She bounced it as if testing its weight. Then she used her thumbs to try prying open the lid. It didn't work. She rapped against the side of the box with her knuckles and held it up to her ear.

"He said don't open it," Emma called.

Tess shot her a furious glare. The other kids turned her way and looked at Emma like she'd just teased a rattlesnake. Emma felt small under Tess's eyes. She'd never seen such hatred in a face before. Her throat closed uncomfortably, and she began to tremble. Obviously this was the effect Tess was searching for. She broke the hard, cold stare and returned her attention to the box.

"Hello!" Tess called, as if speaking to something inside. She laughed quietly. When she had the box lowered from her ear, Tess ran a thumb along its front. Emma couldn't figure out what was going on, or why the box was so important to Justin, but she felt a tangible dread at the thought Tess might actually succeed in opening it. The air thickened with the sensation. The hairs on the back of Emma's neck tingled and danced. She gazed around the room, wondering if anyone else felt what she did, and the look on the other guests' faces told her they did. Everyone had a dull expression of horror, as if watching a car spinning out of control.

Tess Ward yelped a short cry, yanking her hand away from the box. "Damn thing cut me," she said. She brought her thumb to her lips and sucked at the wound. She threw a furious look at Justin as if he'd been the one to cut her.

Then, a nightmare visited Justin Moore's living room.

The lid of the box sprang back, startling Tess Ward so much that she dropped it, sending it crashing to the hardwood floor. Emma held her breath, thinking the thing would break apart on the boards, but it didn't. It landed on its base, lid thrown back, and a silvery cloud rose from the interior.

It looked like thousands of metallic gnats taking to the air at once. They didn't buzz as they rose, but rather crackled like bursts of static electricity. The space between Tess Ward and Justin was soon crawling with the silver specks. Boys in the crowd began to shout, and girls screamed.

"What the hell?"

"Are you seeing this?"

"Oh god. Oh god. Oh god."

A pack of partygoers stampeded for the door as the silvery cloud spread out above Tess Ward's head. It seemed the contents of the box, this cloud of tiny, winged things, was never-ending. Soon, the fireplace and the mantel and the far wall fell under a haze like shimmering dust. A girl Emma didn't know caught her foot on the edge of the carpet as she was trying to flee and flew headlong across the coffee table. She hit with a thud and rolled off into the gap at the foot of the couch. The screaming grew louder as people ran for the door or raced past Emma to take shelter in the kitchen. Her schoolmates fell. Some of them were trampled by other kids trying to get away from the strange aggregation on the far side of the room. Doug and Barry finally released Justin. They scurried back to the wall.

Emma stepped away from the terrifying sight, but she didn't run. It was all too amazing for her to let go of it.

Justin didn't run either. He looked up at the cloud, followed it to the ceiling the way he might look at a fence he intended to climb. Though obviously fasci-nated with the silver specks, Justin stepped back when the cloud rippled, putting space between it and his body.

Tess Ward shrieked as if her skin were being ripped from her bones. Her high-pitched cries cut through the crackling static of the silver swarm. Barely visible through the haze, Tess waved her arms and stomped her feet, never really going anywhere but in constant motion.

Then she collapsed. She just fell over in a dead faint, hitting the boards hard.

Strong hands wrapped around Emma's shoulders, and she found herself being hauled back into the dining room. She didn't want to go, didn't want to lose sight of this amazing event. She fought against the grip, but whoever held her was too strong. When they reached the corner by the kitchen, the hands let loose, and Emma spun.

Russ looked down at her with soft, concerned eyes. His jaw was tight as if he were holding back tears or fury.

"Are you okay?" he asked.

"I think so," Emma replied.

Instead of explaining that she wanted to see what the cloud did, what it became, she simply spun on her heels and ran back to the living room.

"Hey," Russ shouted.

She didn't listen or pause, but when she reached the living room she discovered it was too late. The silver swarm was gone. She looked all over, at the furniture and the floor and the windows and the teens, but there was no sign of the sparkling dust. Justin stood in the middle of the living room, staring down at Tess, who was still unconscious. He looked over his shoulder and saw Emma.

"I . . ." was all he could say.

The box sat on the floor at his feet. It was closed now.

In the distance a muffled explosion sounded. The work crews were blasting the far side of the mountain, causing controlled avalanches so that the accumulated snow didn't crash down on unsuspecting skiers.

From the floor, Tess Ward moaned. It was a horrific sound, wet and harsh like she was choking on blood.

9

Justin stared at the fireplace, not knowing what had happened or what to do about it. The silver cloud was gone. Tess Ward writhed on the floor. He peered at the box and then tore his eyes away from it, fearing a simple glance could reopen the thing and start the madness all over again. Doug and Barry pushed past on their way to help Tess, who made a gargling sound in her throat.

The two boys knelt down.

"Serve me," Tess Ward said.

Justin felt certain he'd misheard her request. Surely she'd said "Help me" or some such plea but his rattled mind had altered the girl's words.

Doug and Barry lifted Tess by the arms, helping her to her feet.

"You shouldn't move her," a quiet voice suggested. It was the new girl, the girl he'd flirted with when "personally inviting" her to the party: Emma. "We don't know what happened. She might have hit her head when she fainted. Let's just wait for an ambulance to get here."

"No," Tess snapped. She shook loose from the two boys and faced Emma. "I think I've been humiliated enough for one night." Tess made a grand show of looking around the room, while the two boys stood beside her, confused. "I like your house, Justin. I'll be sure my father asks for it in the settlement."

A spike of fear pierced Justin's chest. "I told you to leave the box alone."

He waited for Tess's response, his nerves rattling like a diamondback's tail.

Tess's face went pale and her mouth sagged at the corners. Justin thought she might keel over again, and he stepped forward. Then her eyes cleared, became sharp and hard like the edges of a knife, and she stood straight-backed.

"You don't tell me anything," Tess said.

There was something different about her voice. It was lower and carried a dreadful wet intonation like she was again trying to breathe through blood. The sound of it chilled him, struck him as wholly wrong. Doug and Barry must have noticed it too. They moved away from Tess, only one cautious step each. The fall must have really hurt her, Justin thought. Was she bleeding internally?

What is Pops going to do to me when he finds out about this?

"Take me home," Tess ordered.

Doug and Barry reached out and took an arm each. Slowly, they led Tess through the living room and into the entryway. They passed the few kids who had not fled, a handful of boys and girls cowering by the coat closet. Their pace was slow and smooth. Between the two boys, Tess seemed to glide more than walk. It was a royal procession, a regal exit. The sight of it in the aftermath of the silver swarm was disturbing in the extreme.

All of the air in the room seemed to follow them, and Justin found it hard to breathe. His heart thumped loudly against his ribs.

Doug opened the door. Justin noticed that it had begun snowing outside. Then Tess passed over the threshold, the door closed, and Justin could breathe again.

"Are you okay?" Emma asked.

She'd walked up behind him. Her question startled him, and he spun on her.

"What?" he asked, still disoriented.

"Are you okay?"

"I-I think so," he replied, but the trembling in his

voice made a more truthful statement about his head space. "I just don't know what happened."

"What is that thing?" Emma asked, pointing at the box. "Where did it come from?"

"One of the blast crews found it in a cave." His party guests—those who hadn't fled at the first sight of the swarm—began to gather in the living room. "No one was supposed to touch it. That's why I hid it. I told her to leave it alone."

He was starting to panic. He felt waves of it running through his muscles and bones; he heard it flavoring his voice. A dozen kids stared at him, and all of them wore questions on their faces, but he didn't have any answers.

"What if it was poisonous?" a girl asked from the back of the room. She'd hopped on the panic bus herself. Already her eyes were wild and her hands flapped beside her as if she'd just touched something gross. "What if it was some kind of disease?"

"It wasn't a disease," Emma said loudly. "And I doubt it was poison."

"It could have been," the girl replied. "It could have been *nuc-lar* or something. I could be dying right now."

The girl burst into tears. She ran for the front door,

her hands still flapping at her sides like impotent wings with which she wanted to fly away.

Three boys, gamer geeks by the look of them, tore out of the house after the girl. The remaining teens continued to stare at Justin, but where there had been questions on their faces, he now saw only anger.

"Dude, if you poisoned us I am so kicking your ass," Brian Knott said. He was the star of the school's basketball team, and Justin knew he could follow through on his threat.

"What kind of a dickhead keeps something like that lying around the house?" Kevin Taylor asked.

"Idiot," another boy said.

The verbal abuse continued. Justin didn't know what to say or do. Brian Knott decided that a vocal threat wasn't enough, so he walked up and shoved Justin hard.

"If anything happens to me," Brian reiterated, "you're dead."

"He told her to leave the box alone," Emma said. "If you're going to be pissed off at anyone, be pissed off at Tess. Justin didn't do anything wrong."

Brian looked shocked that anyone would interrupt his intimidation. He faced off on Emma, scowling. With his index finger he jabbed Justin's chest, turning

65

his head at a predatory angle. "Dead," he repeated.

Brian stalked out of the living room. He walked down the hall to retrieve his coat from the guest-room bed and slammed the door on his way out of the house. The other kids followed.

After a few minutes, only four guests remained. Emma was back in the dining area, talking to Russ Foster, shaking her head and trying to smile. Emma's friend, Betina, looked annoyed as she listened to something Kit Urban was telling her.

"At least the party was memorable," Justin announced as he wandered up to Emma and her friends.

"It wasn't your fault," Emma told him.

"Yeah, man," Kit said. "Like many of the world's evils, Tess was the source."

Russ didn't say anything. He just glared at Justin.

"Personally, I'd buy you flowers if you managed to weed out a few of the Cools," Betina added dryly.

"Betina!" Emma said.

"Well, it's not like he actually poisoned them," Betina argued.

"Then what did happen?" Russ asked. "I mean, come on, we all saw it. Something came out of *that* box. And for that matter, where the hell did it go?"

"It probably dissipated," Emma offered.

"Dissipated?" Betina shook her head. "Sorry, but that wasn't fog."

"Moore," Russ said earnestly, "you were standing right there. What happened to that shit?"

Justin couldn't say for certain. He'd been so transfixed by the ominous swarm, its vanishing had taken him by surprise. All he could remember was looking at the fireplace through the haze, and suddenly, it was gone.

"Well?" Russ insisted.

"I don't know," Justin said. "It must have gone back in the box."

"So you're saying it's alive?" Russ asked. "Great. Now *I'm* worried about disease."

"Nanobots," Kit said. He was totally serious.

"Nano-huh?"

"Like these übersmall computers, right? You read about them all the time."

"Only if you're a sci-fi geek," Russ said.

"We all saw the stuff. It was silvery, right? Maybe the cloud was sentient." Kit looked around to see if anyone knew what he was talking about. Justin sure didn't. "That means it can think. Maybe that box is really an alien pod of some kind, and that swarm . . ."

"Give it a rest," Russ said, exasperated. "This wasn't an alien invasion, brain damage, it was probably just some trapped gas. Moore here said some guys found the box in a cave. A kid probably buried his pet guinea pig up there a hundred years ago, and when the air hit it, poof!"

"Like those mummies we saw on the Discovery Channel," Kit said. "Maybe it was cursed."

"Great," Betina said, "now we're discussing Fluffy Ho-Tep. Emma, it's time to go."

"Shouldn't we help clean up?"

Justin realized he should say something. He should tell them it was okay. He could clean up himself, but he didn't want to be alone in the house, alone with the box. He wanted them to stay, especially Emma.

They were all looking at him now. He tried to smile to show them he was okay, but the smile weighed too much, and he couldn't hold it.

"No," he said finally. "I'll clean up. You guys take off."

"Are you sure?" Emma asked.

"Totally. Thanks for coming out. Sorry for the crisis."

"It wasn't your fault," Emma said.

She really is cool, Justin thought. He wished he'd spent more time talking to her tonight. He'd thought she was hot from the first moment he saw her, but now he felt like he could really like her—if she ever talked to him again.

He led the remaining guests down the hall so they could get their coats. At the front door, he took a long last look at Emma as she waved from the edge of the driveway before climbing into Betina's car. *Yeah, she was cool.*

Justin closed the door and observed the aftermath of the party. His anxiety knotted and twisted tighter. His pops was going to kill him. Tess Ward was going to sue him. Every kid in the school hated him.

Great party, he thought. *Good job, sport.*

10

Word traveled fast in Winter, Colorado.

The following morning, Emma went to school as she normally did, but there was nothing normal about the day. Everyone on the bus was talking about what had happened at Justin's party, even kids who hadn't been there. The school's chat room had filled up after the tragic bash, and the stories went from bizarre to absolutely stupid.

It was some fungus his dad smuggled in from China.

It was a bioweapon he stole from the government.

It was a ghost he bought off the internet, like in that book.

Emma thought Kit's theory about intelligent alien computer dust was sounding a lot more logical. Betina wrote the whole thing off as group hysteria.

"I mean, we were waiting for something to happen," she said. "That whole standoff between Tess and Justin cranked things up a notch, and bam! The box opened and our collective unconscious flew out of it."

"Okay," Emma said, "but what caused the cloud?

What was in that box?"

"How do you even know it came out of the box?" Betina asked. "They were standing by the fireplace. Maybe they left the flue open and a gust of wind sent a cloud of ash into the room."

"Ash doesn't reflect light. The cloud was silver, and it was more like a swarm than a cloud. Didn't you hear the static in the air?"

"No, actually, I didn't. Maybe that was something you projected on it."

"I don't think so," Emma said.

"The fact is, we may never know. More than likely, Russ was right—and that is not a sentence I ever thought I'd utter. But still, if something is sealed up for a long time and it hits the air, it can vaporize."

Emma let the conversation end. She didn't accept Betina's explanation any more than she accepted the idea that Justin's dad had smuggled a mutant mushroom in from Asia. She remembered the swarm, remembered its metallic glint, would never forget the way it hovered in the air as if waiting for direction. If she concentrated, she could still hear the crackling noise it made, like a thousand tiny pops in the air.

At school, the full effects of the rumor machine were apparent. Every conversation was about Justin's party. Kids she didn't even know came up to her and asked what had happened.

But things got even weirder in first period, when she heard about Tess Ward. The news came from Laney Hoffman, a wired-up Cool with long, kinky red hair and skin like milk.

"I'm so not joking," Laney was saying when Emma walked into the classroom.

Out of reflex, Emma looked at the fourth row to see if Russ had arrived, but he was nowhere to be seen. She walked down the aisle to her seat, checking out Laney and her audience.

The girl sat in the far row. Behind her was a bank of windows. Snowflakes drifted through the gray morning haze. Laney's audience was made up of ten guys and girls, all turned toward the redhead, eyes and ears wide to take in as much dirt as Laney had for them.

"She was just stumbling around the streets. Vic saw her when he came into town last night."

"Who's Vic?" Emma asked Betina.

"Laney's brother. He plays guitar for some folk-pop group. It's audio abuse of the highest level."

". . . He was coming back from Denver and the icy roads slowed him down, so he didn't get into town until like three in the morning, and he saw Tess wandering down Corporal Street, looking tweaked out of her mind."

"Do you think it was because of what happened at the party?"

"Uh, no," Laney said. "We were all at the party. Did you get a buzz? I didn't get a buzz, and I was standing like right in the middle of that stuff."

"She wasn't even in the living room," Emma told Betina.

"She's trashing Tess. I'll forgive her anything."

Laney looked up at Emma and Betina. Likely she hadn't heard what they were saying but was still annoyed that they felt anything they could say to each other was half as important as the story she was telling.

"Anyway," Laney said, drawing her audience in. "Vic stopped and asked if Tess needed a lift home. I mean, it was like ten degrees outside, and he said she was walking around in nothing but that little dress she wore to the party."

"She could have frozen to death," Deb Kirby said.

"She may have," Laney said. "She wouldn't let Vic take her home. She told him that she had work to do, that her work was just beginning. Right? How totally asylum-worthy is that? He knew she was fried, so he left her there. He called nine-one-one, and they probably dragged her off to rehab. Whatev. All I know is she isn't answering her cell, and she wasn't at the coffee stand this morning."

"Oh my god," Deb gushed, covering her mouth as if hearing a family member had died on the operating table. "Aren't you worried?"

"Devastated," Laney said. "She was my best friend, but after last night . . . I mean, how can I hang with her now? It would be totally humiliating for us both."

"What a bitch," Betina whispered with a laugh.

"Do you think she's telling the truth about Tess?" Emma asked.

"Who knows? She left with Doug and Barry. They aren't above slipping roofies. In fact, I think it falls right after 'bring flowers' on their dating checklist."

"I hope she's okay."

"You wouldn't if you knew her," Betina replied. "I swear, if evil has a face, it is Tess Ward's face."

Emma was sitting in Mr. Dickinson's English lit class when the vice principal's voice rolled from the school's public address speakers. She had been looking out the window at the ever-increasing snowfall, and the tone that announced PA messages startled her.

"Due to inclement weather, classes will be excused immediately following fourth period. The national weather bureau has issued blizzard warnings for the county. School buses have been dispatched and will make all required stops. For those of you who need to arrange for rides, please feel free to use your cell phones in the hallways after fourth-period classes. An announcement has been issued via email to all parents registered on the school's contact list. Enjoy your winter break."

Whoops and exclamations of appreciation accompanied the announcement. In fact, Emma could hardly hear the message that followed the vice principal's opening sentence. Everyone in the class was beaming, except for Mr. Dickinson. He just looked relieved.

"You're not free yet," the teacher said. "Let's go over a few points regarding the book reports you handed in. The quality of the compositions was generally migraine producing. I dread the idea that some of you are eligible to vote, though I take some comfort in the knowledge you are too lazy to do so. After my headache subsided, I returned to the pile and found a few examples of competent composition. However, the majority of you . . ."

Wham!

The sound made Emma jump and spin around in her chair to see what had caused it. In the back of the room, Barry Lebbon lifted his palm and again slammed it down on the desk.

Wham!

Emma had noticed Barry when she'd first started at McKinley, because he was built like an Abercrombie & Fitch model, one of the really good ones they used in the beach layouts. After his behavior last night, holding Justin so Tess could tease and threaten him, Emma was glad she hadn't wasted any time on the boy.

Barry lifted his palm and slapped the desktop a third time. *Wham!*

"Mr. Lebbon," the teacher said, "do you have a problem?"

Barry shot out of his seat and threw his desk against the back wall. "I have a problem," the boy said ferociously. He stomped along the aisle toward the front of the class, directly at Mr. Dickinson. "And now, I'm thinking you got a problem too."

With no further warning, Barry threw a fist at the teacher's face. Showing surprising agility, Mr. Dickinson rolled backward over his desk, avoiding the punch. A girl screamed and the whole class was on its feet, shouting or laughing, depending on how the incident struck them. Fortunately, Mr. Dickinson was quick. Emma couldn't tell if the teacher had gotten lucky or if he was really that graceful, but it looked like a perfectly coordinated stunt, until he tried to regain his footing behind the desk and slipped. Barry took the opportunity and circled around to continue his attack on the teacher.

"Mr. Lebbon!" the teacher shouted, using the desk to support his weight as he struggled to his feet. "Do not force me to subdue you."

"Try it, fat ass, and I'll rip your throat out with my teeth," Barry replied, spit flying from his lips. "You and your reports. Flunking me! You think you're going to flunk me?"

Barry tried to land a punch to the teacher's stomach, but Dickinson leaped back.

Gasps and shrill cries filled the class. One kid near the back cackled crazily as if the scene was the funniest thing he'd ever seen.

"I am forced by law to tell you that I am a black belt in—" Mr. Dickinson didn't finish the sentence because Barry yanked a coffee mug from the teacher's desk and hurled it at his head. Dickinson ducked as the ceramic cup flew against the far wall, shattering into a hundred pieces.

"Oh, screw this," Dickinson said. He skipped forward and landed a kick to Barry's groin. When the boy doubled over, the teacher performed a strange yet graceful spinning kick to his face, sending Barry facedown on the linoleum. The teacher backed away from the prone student and pulled his cell phone from the pocket of his Dockers. He punched three buttons, then hit Send.

"Jeez-usssss," Betina said. "Was that for real?"

"I think it was very real," Emma replied. She could barely hear with all the blood rushing to her ears. Her pulse thudded like bass drums. She felt dizzy with adrenaline.

"Hello, yes, this is John Dickinson at McKinley High," the teacher said. "I'm going to need an ambulance and the police. . . . Didn't I just say McKinley High School? . . . Then wouldn't it make sense to send them here? . . . I'm reporting an assault. . . . The perpetrator is named Barry Lebbon, and he's seventeen years old. . . . Right now? . . . Right now, he's facedown on the floor, bleeding. . . ." Dickinson looked up from his call. "You're excused," he said as if it was the most obvious thing in the world. "Go on, get out of here. Go to the library and read a book. I suggest something about self-defense." He returned his attention to the call. "Yes. Yes, I'm still here."

Emma and Betina joined the flow of students filing out of the room, all of them putting as much distance as possible between themselves and the scene at the front of the class. Adrenaline still buzzed through Emma's system and she found herself wired on the stuff.

"I don't believe this," she muttered.

"Surreal and violent," Betina said. "And yet even I am having a difficult time finding the joy in this situation."

"What happened? Barry was like insane."

"No kidding. Thank god we're done with this place for a couple of weeks. These people are nuts."

Or they're going *nuts*, Emma thought.

She thought about a silver swarm. Popping static. Her skin pimpled as if freezing.

11

Justin was glad to see Emma walking toward him. Though white as a ghost, she was a friendly face among many enemies. All morning he'd endured slashing glares and sneers. Kids pointing. Shaking their heads. When the vice principal had announced that school was closing, a flood of relief washed over him. This feeling only increased when he saw Emma. Her class had been excused early too.

His bio class was let go because the teacher, Mrs. Friedhoff, couldn't be bothered to lecture. She'd sat in the class for twenty minutes after the bell rang, saying nothing, barely moving, just staring at the floor. After the vice principal's announcement, Mrs. Friedhoff lifted her head as if it weighed a hundred pounds, gazed around, and dismissed the class. Though many of Justin's classmates celebrated with laughter and high fives, he walked out of class with a creepy feeling on the back of his neck.

Emma waved at him, and Justin walked over to her and Betina.

"What happened?" Emma asked.

"I was about to ask you the same question."

She told him about Barry Lebbon's meltdown and the way Mr. Dickinson subdued the guy with a couple of karate moves. Justin couldn't believe what he was hearing, but the haunted look on Emma's face and Betina's nodding agreement convinced him of the story's truth. He told them about Mrs. Friedhoff.

"I'm voting we bail now," Betina said. "No point hanging around the halls for the next thirty minutes."

"Gets my vote," Justin said.

"Are we allowed to just go?" Emma asked quietly.

"Why not?" Justin said. "Do you guys need anything from your lockers?"

He led them down the hall and made a right into the long corridor of lockers leading to the lobby. They each stopped and put away their books, grabbed their coats and gloves. Justin closed the metal door of his locker with a sharp *clang*.

Tess Ward entered the far end of the hall, startling him. She still wore the dress she'd had on the night before. Her tread was soft but jerking, as if the floor were collapsing beneath her every step. She didn't seem to even notice Justin or the others. She just walked as if in a trance toward a door marked Teachers' Lounge.

"Crap," he whispered. What had happened to her?

"Was that Tess?" Emma asked, sidling up to him.

"Yeah, I think so."

"Well, she wasn't looking too homecoming queen, was she?" Betina said.

"We should help her," Emma suggested. "Something's really wrong. I mean, if what Laney said is true, she's been up all night."

"What are we supposed to do?" Justin asked. Honestly, he didn't want to help her. He didn't want to be anywhere near her.

"We can talk to her," Emma said. "We can keep an eye on her until an ambulance arrives."

"Okay," Justin said. He sighed out a lungful of air and set off down the hall. "I warned her about that box."

"I don't think this is about the box," Emma said.

"I think it's about meth and diet pills," Betina added. "I sort of *want* it to be about meth and diet pills."

"Betina, please," Emma said.

As they approached the door to the teachers' lounge, Justin felt his legs slowing down. He didn't want to go in the room. He didn't want to have to face Tess Ward, not after what had happened at his party.

It wasn't his fault, and she wasn't his problem. She was a spoiled rich girl who expected everyone else to pay for her screwups. Expected everyone to fall down and forgive because she was a privileged bitch and guys thought she was hot. Justin knew he had a lot in common with Tess, but he never messed with people to make himself grin, and he certainly didn't blame other people for his crap.

Emma walked around him and hurried for the door, apparently eager to help Tess. Betina scurried past him as well. Emma opened the door and then recoiled, startling Justin and sending his heart to a rapid thumping.

"Oh, hell," Betina gasped.

What now? Justin wondered as he stepped over the threshold.

The teachers' lounge was a large room. Near the door where they stood, two small green sofas faced each other across a narrow wooden coffee table. Farther back stood a large round table circled by eight molded plastic chairs the color of wheat. Against the back wall a kitchen-like area had been built. There was a refrigerator, a sink, a small stove, and a slender counter running in an L-shape at the corner. Tess Ward stood facing this corner, but she wasn't alone.

She was kissing someone, or trying to.

Mr. Reed, the shop teacher, leaned back against the counter, trying to escape Tess's advances. The teacher's fat, hairy hands gripped Tess's shoulders, trying to push her away.

Justin couldn't help but remember the mating moves Tess had tried on him the night before. They hadn't been nearly this desperate, but he understood the shop teacher's struggle.

"Gross redefined," Betina said.

"Get her away from me," the shop teacher yelled.

The plea seemed to be unnecessary; apparently, Tess was done with him. She stepped back and let him slide away along the counter. Once free of the girl, Mr. Reed waddled like an enormous, terrified penguin to the exit.

Tess continued facing the corner away from them. Justin noticed her dress was ruined, stained and torn. A smudge of mud, like a football-shaped scab, ran over the fabric at the hip.

"Tess?" Emma said, stepping forward. "Tess, are you okay?"

"Fine," she replied. Justin noticed the low, wet sound in her voice, and cold fingers ran down his back. "So . . . very . . . fine."

Justin reached out and grabbed Emma's shoulder, not wanting her to get too close. His caution was warranted, as became terribly apparent when Tess turned to face them across the teachers' lounge.

Tess's once beautiful face was altered; it was grotesque. Sharp cheekbones accentuated sunken cheeks and eyes. Shadows filled the gaunt recesses. Her lips were cracked and swollen. Her skin was the color of bacon fat and shimmered beneath a slick of sweat. She looked horrible. She looked dead.

"Tess," Emma whispered, her voice cracking with emotion.

The hideous face moved up and down, bobbing fluidly as if moving to some unseen music. A speck of silver appeared at the corner of Tess's mouth; it shimmered for a moment, then took to the air, circling her head like a gnat.

Oh, man, Justin thought. Whatever those silver things were, some had gotten into Tess. It looked like they'd been eating away at her from the inside, leaving nothing but skin and bones.

"Oh, man," he said aloud, feeling thick guilt working through his veins as the stricken girl continued to nod her head. "Oh, man."

He backed away until he felt the doorjamb

between his shoulder blades.

Then the dazed expression on Tess's face burned away beneath a flash of sudden excitement. "You have the vessel," she said. "My vessel." Tess stepped forward. "Give it to me."

"What is she talking about?" Emma asked.

Justin didn't care. He only wanted to be away from Tess. Far, far away. "Come on," he said. "Come on. Come on. Let's go!"

Justin started the Range Rover's engine. A blast of cold air poured through the vents, washing over him and adding to his chill. The sky above was steel gray with wisps of black running like veins through the angry clouds. Snow fell in a thick haze. He couldn't even see the street at the far side of the parking lot through the dense weather. It had been plowed late the night before but the morning's snowfall had already turned it white again. Next to him, Emma shivered in the passenger seat. Betina sat quietly behind them. He checked her reflection in the rearview and saw her working the edge of her thumbnail between her teeth.

"Where are we going?" he asked. "Should I take you home?"

"My mom's at work," Emma said.

She doesn't want to be alone, Justin thought. He couldn't blame her.

"Mine too," Betina added quietly.

"Well, we should stay together," he said. "I mean, at least until your parents get home. Maybe by then someone will know what's going on."

"It was the box," Emma said. "Whatever came out of that box is causing this."

Justin had been thinking the same thing, but he'd kept quiet. His feelings of guilt had been at full throttle since seeing Tess in the teachers' lounge. He blamed himself for the terrible changes to her once beautiful face. He blamed himself for a lot of things. Barry Lebbon had been at the party. He'd held Justin while Tess played with the box; both Barry and Tess were right there when that swarm rose to fill the air. It couldn't be a coincidence that they'd both gone postal.

"We're okay," Betina said from the backseat. "We were right there, and nothing happened to us."

"She's right," Justin said, finding a sliver of hope in Betina's words. He'd been as close to the swarm as anyone, and he wasn't freaking out. Maybe Tess and Barry went out partying after they left his place. They could have gotten their hands on some tainted X or any number of celebratory chemicals. It could have happened, but Justin didn't believe it. Recreational drugs couldn't explain the silver remnant from the swarm emerging from Tess's mouth.

"Nothing's happened to us, *yet*," Emma said. "And maybe it won't, but this isn't a coincidence. Do you have any idea what that thing is?"

"What? No. Like I said, my dad brought it home. One of the work crews found it in a cave after blasting the mountainside. Nobody knew what it was." But he remembered someone was coming this afternoon for the box. A professor from Denver University, who was supposed to be an expert. Justin hoped the guy would make it through the storm.

"Turn on the radio," Betina said.

"The radio?" Justin asked. He leaned over and punched the on button. A barrage of guitar and drums poured from the speakers. Quickly, he adjusted the volume. "What do you want to hear?"

"How about the news?" Betina suggested. "It might be a good idea to know what's going on."

"Oh, right," Justin replied, feeling stupid. "What channel?" he asked.

"I'll find it," Emma said. "You keep your eyes on the road."

As voices and snippets of tunes flashed through the speakers, Justin drove toward the village. They'd never decided on a destination. Holing up at a restaurant might be the best plan. He could certainly use some coffee.

A low, serious voice came over the speakers. The reporter discussed a new scientific study about global warming, which struck Justin as bizarre considering he was driving through a blizzard. Finally, after another report about the new president, the weather report came on.

"Persistent blizzard conditions result in the closing of a number of mountain passes. An avalanche outside of Winter, Colorado, has shut down Walker Pass. Work crews are on the scene and expect the accumulation to be cleared by late this afternoon. Winter storm warnings remain in effect for the counties of . . ."

The news sank into his already uneasy thoughts. Dread sparked in the back of his head and radiated out in hot waves.

"Did he just say we were trapped in this town?" Justin asked.

12

Russ stood against a glass display case in the school's lobby. Inside the case was a collection of awards for academics and sports—ribbons, trophies, certificates, and photographs of grinning kids. Classmates swarmed through the lobby, many of them chatting happily about the early onset of winter break. They came in waves. Some looked worried, upset. Maybe it had something to do with the paramedics Russ had seen in the hallway earlier. Kit had heard that Barry Lebbon lost it and went postal on one of the teachers.

In front of him, Kit paced furiously, head down, cell phone nestled into his long blond hair.

"Not cool, Mom," Kit was saying. "Not cool."

Russ searched the faces of the exiting students, hoping to see Emma, but he never saw her. He'd woken up late that morning, after having been up most of the night thinking about her and that Justin kid's party. Normally staying up late wasn't a big deal. His dad always woke him up by crashing around the kitchen or closing the front door too loudly as he transitioned from running the plow at night to his job working the tram cars. This morning, however, no such disturbances cut through his sleep. When he did wake to the sound of Kit's bleating car horn, he'd been disoriented. He hurried into some clothes and raced through the kitchen to the front door, waving for Kit to come inside while he got ready. After Kit joined him in the house, Russ noticed that his father hadn't made coffee, and he wondered if the old man had even come home between jobs.

By the time he'd showered and dressed, they'd already missed first period—missed calculus class and Emma. He hadn't even seen her in the halls between classes. He'd hoped to get her email address before the break, maybe see if she was up for a movie or dinner or something. But the students kept flowing past him, and Emma wasn't among them.

Laney Hoffman, surrounded by half a dozen Cools, looked over at him with her usual disdain. A speck of glitter shimmered on her cheek just below her eye. It caught the light, twinkling for a moment. Then it seemed to move up her face in a way that made Russ feel decidedly uneasy. A moment later, Laney was past him, moving through the front doors of McKinley High and into the gray whirl outside.

"Okay, Mom," Kit said, "but this blows." He folded the phone and shoved it in the pocket of his shorts. "No board today," he said in frustration.

"Oh, man." Russ had hoped they could take advantage of the early closing and get in a couple hours of snowboarding before the real storm hit. "What's up?"

"I have to pick up my sisters," Kit said. "And then my mom wants me to watch them until she gets home. So *not* cool. Like when did I become a babysitter?"

"We can hang at your place and play some Xbox."

"Can't, dude. I also have chores. Look, let me drop you off at home. I'll handle this festival of suckage and then we can figure out what to do. Mom's going to be home around four."

By then, the blizzard would be full-blown, Russ knew. Kit might not even be able to drive over in it.

"Crap," Russ said, suddenly less happy about the school closure. "Okay. Well, let's get out of here."

They walked through the front doors of the school into the icy air. Laney stood in the center of a pack of kids on the front walk, some Cools, some dregs. All of the students looked gray, as if the snowfall had bleached the color from them. Russ paused, taking in this strange crowd. A moment later, the school's doors opened again and Tess appeared.

Man, she looked ragged. Russ squinted because he couldn't believe how much her appearance had changed in a little more than twelve hours. Even the way she moved was wrong, her steps uneven as if she had just learned to walk. She emerged into the storm, wearing nothing but a thin dress. She continued forward to the crowd surrounding Laney. The kids parted for her, engulfed her.

The whole thing creeped Russ out bad, and he backed away. He turned and ran to catch up with Kit, who had wandered toward the parking lot by himself.

In the car Kit ranted about his mother's instructions. Of course it was another conspiracy. According to Kit, his parents wanted to force him into compliance, preparing him for the only future they understood.

"They brainwash us young, right?" Kit said. "They figure if they impose all of these rules on us now, we'll get used to being subservient bitches, so we won't cause trouble when the corporate god shoves us into a cubicle and makes us sacrifice our souls for a paycheck."

"Yeah, I'm sure that's it," Russ said, humored.

Where did Kit come up with this crap?

"You know, that's the problem with you, dude," Kit said. "You don't believe in anything. You don't fight for anything. It's all like, 'Whatever. Can't change the world.'"

"Lighten up, man. You're just pissed at your mom and you're taking it out on me."

"No way. I've totally been thinking about this. You think I'm this wacko because I look beneath the surface of things, look for the gears that turn society and point out the ones that are rusted and broken. You just accept things. I mean, are you really that empty?"

"I'm not empty. What the hell does that even mean? And for the record, I think you're wacko because you're wacko, man. That's it."

Kit didn't immediately respond. He drove them around a bend in the road and made a right. They began the descent into the village of Winter. Laid out along Main Street, the downtown ran for eight blocks before the road again angled up, leading to the forested peaks where rich people, like that guy Justin, lived. Though he couldn't see it, Russ knew that on the right a sharp ridge rose behind a low residential area. Beyond the ridge were the ski slopes and the new resort hotel where Emma's mom worked.

They cruised into downtown and the shadowy side of a three-story building rose on the right. The building housed a drugstore and a pet shop on the first floor. The upper floors were cut up into apartments. Lights ran over the awning on the front of the building. At least the power was still on. Many of the shops were lit up, and the streetlamps worked, casting yellow ghosts against the field of gray and white, but these dull illuminations only served to further point out the emptiness of the village. With the snow, it looked like a ghost town filmed through static.

"Where is everyone?" Kit asked.

"Inside," Russ replied. "Where it's warm."

"No way," Kit argued. "Something's wrong. Something is totally whacked here. Ever since the party last night I've felt it, totally felt it in my bones. Tess unleashed something, dude. You wait and see. Did you hear the roads out of town are blocked?"

"Kit, this is a mountain town, and avalanches happen. Streets get closed. People like being warm, and blizzards don't scream comfy, so they stay indoors. These aren't signs of the apocalypse. It's just another winter in Winter."

As he spoke, Russ noticed a shadowy form pull away from one of the buildings and run into the street.

At first, he'd thought it was a fat guy hurrying to his car, but the figure didn't stop at the curb and when it charged into the beams of Kit's headlights, he saw a man and a woman engaged in a violent argument. She was slapping at the man and kicking at his shins. Kit slammed on the brakes. The tires skidded and slipped over the low snow pack, but eventually grabbed. The couple paused in their argument long enough to throw furious glances at him; then they continued to the far sidewalk.

"Does that look normal to you?" Kit asked. He looked at Russ for an answer, but something outside the passenger side of the car caught his attention. "Or that?" Kit pointed.

Russ turned to the passenger window. Beyond it, in the fudge shop beside Revens Ski Supply, a tall kid with scraggly blond hair frantically shoved handfuls of candy into his mouth as he pounded on the glass of a display counter with his other hand. The elderly woman behind the counter looked freaked. She grabbed more fudge from a tray and set it in front of the boy. Before her hand had withdrawn, the blond kid snatched at the candy. He slapped the woman's hand in the process. She danced away from him as he shoved the fresh batch of sweets into his chocolate-stained mouth.

"That's Vic Hoffman, dude. Laney's brother."

Russ had to admit the guy's desperation for fudge was over the top. Still, it wasn't like people were rising from the dead. It wasn't like they were swarming houses and eating people. They weren't dropping dead on the sidewalks. Probably just a few people getting a little crazy because a storm was coming in. The winter had already been a hard one. A lot of snow.

It wasn't a big deal.

"A chocoholic dosing up before the blizzard hits doesn't exactly signal the end of the world."

"Sure, and a kid going postal in class doesn't signal the end of the world, and a bunch of metal dust erupting from a freaky box doesn't signal the end of the world, but you start putting these things together and it means something. It's all connected."

"How can it be connected? Vic wasn't even at the party."

"See, dude, that's what I'm talking about. You never question anything. You just lie back and accept things the way they look."

"As opposed to accepting conspiracy theories and fairy tales?"

"Dude, you're like hopeless. You're like an ostrich, man. Head in the dirt. You won't fight for anything."

"Whatever, man," Russ said. "It's not like I've got a hell of a lot to fight for."

13

Emma shivered. She still wore her coat. She held a mug of steaming tea in her hands. The heat in the house worked just fine and Justin had started a fire in the fireplace, but she could not get warm. She hugged herself tightly and pushed into the thick cushions of the sofa.

"You want to try calling your mom again?" Betina asked, offering her cell phone.

Emma shook her head. She'd already tried five times and no one was answering at the hotel. Her mother's cell phone was sending calls directly to voice mail.

"We'll be okay here," Justin said, jabbing at the logs on the hearth with an iron poker. "We have plenty to eat, and if that guy from the university made it through before the avalanche, he might be able to tell us what that box is. If it's responsible for what happened to Tess, he might know how to stop it."

Emma watched Justin tend the fire. His presence comforted her. He was totally cool and strong. She was glad she hadn't gone home to the empty duplex.

Betina's cell phone rang, and Emma turned expectantly, hoping the call was from her mother. It was.

"Oh honey, I'm so sorry," her mom said. "I turned my cell off last night while it was charging and didn't think to turn it back on. It'd still be off, but I needed to call the seafood distributor. The prices he's quoted for shrimp are just ridiculous. We'd have to—"

"Mom," Emma interrupted. "Did you listen to my messages?"

"Of course I did. Well, the first one. That's how I knew you were at this number. Drake was talking the whole time, of course, so I didn't hear every single word, but we're talking now. And why *are* we talking right now, young lady? Aren't you supposed to be in class?"

Typical, her mother hadn't heard a single word she'd said. She probably hadn't listened to Emma's messages, either, just called back the number in her missed call list. "Look, Mom, this is important. Something's going on. School was dismissed early, but before they let us out, this kid lost it."

"Lost what?"

"He freaked out, okay? A violent outburst, but that's not all."

"Outbursts? Honey, what are you talking about? Is someone at school picking on you?"

"No, Mom. Jeez, I'm not in the third grade." Emma heard a man's voice over the line. It must have been Drake, her mother's assistant chef. He was babbling about seafood and sounded ready to scream. "Mom? This is serious. Are you listening?"

"Yes, honey. Of course I am."

"It's like this kid just went crazy for no reason."

"Well, there has to be a reason, honey."

"Look," Emma said, "I'm at a friend's house. Call me when you get off work and I'll come home then."

"Well, I'll be late. They just closed the tram because of the blizzard. I'm going to have to ride back to the village with Drake, and he tells me it can take an hour in bad weather."

"Just call me," Emma said.

"I'll be fine, honey," her mother said. "We'll talk about that mean boy later."

Emma punched the end button, shook her head in exasperation, and tossed the cell back to Betina. "It's like talking to a television set."

"At least you know she's okay," Justin said. He crossed to the sofa and sat down between the girls.

"I just wish I knew what happened to Tess and

Barry, you know?" Emma said.

"Whatever it is," Justin said, "there's nothing we can do about it. By now the police will be involved. They'll handle it."

"You'd think they'd have a report about Barry on the television or radio. You can't stub your toe in a public school without it making the five o'clock news."

"No local stations," Betina said. "The closest is probably in Montrose. Besides, they can't get camera crews out here and if they don't have pictures, it's not real news."

"And it may not be that bad," Justin said. "I mean, Barry freaked. It could just be cabin fever or something."

"Tess was not suffering from cabin fever," Emma pointed out.

"No," Betina said, "she was up all night, tweaking."

"Even that doesn't explain the way she looked," Emma argued. "She'd have to have been tweaking for a month to look that sick."

"I told you she had the face of evil."

"Betina, this isn't funny. She's really sick."

"Duh," Betina replied. "And I'm scared, and the fear is manifesting itself as inappropriate humor, plus

I'm trying to make sense out of a seemingly senseless situation, which is why I'm identifying real-world possibilities to which I can attribute the source of my fear."

Emma and Justin looked at Betina, speechless. She returned their gazes and shrugged.

"My parents forced me to take therapy last year," she said. "Even my therapist said I was painfully self-aware."

Emma couldn't argue with her. She'd always thought Betina was smart, a lot smarter than most of their classmates.

"For now, let's just chill," Justin said. "We've got beverages and a fire. We can watch a movie or play some video games. Whatever."

Emma liked Justin, and she didn't want to contradict him, but that was the dumbest thing she'd ever heard. They should be watching the news, surfing the Web for information. She trembled, still cold. Holding her mug of tea carefully, she leaned forward and stood from the sofa.

"Is it okay if I check email on your computer?" she asked. "I should send a note to my dad." She didn't really need to send a note to her father. He was thousands of miles away, and there was nothing he could do. But she thought if she got online, she'd run across a news piece — or maybe some of the kids from school were blogging about what had happened. She didn't want to just tune everything out, because if things got worse, she wanted to be prepared for it.

"Sure." Justin rose from the sofa. He set off across the room and led her toward the hall.

Betina also stood from the sofa and followed.

Justin's room amazed Emma. It was huge, easily the size of the living room in the apartment she shared with her mother. A flat-panel, high-def television hung from the wall, like a great nickel-framed window opening onto a dismally gray sky. Beneath it, a glass and wrought-iron entertainment center held a DVD player, an audio tuner, and an Xbox 360 console. Justin's bed was positioned against the wall on the far side of the room, under a window that looked out onto a paler yet equally dismal grayness. Another flat-panel screen, his computer monitor, sat alone on the bleached-pine desk. No papers, pens, or pencils cluttered the surface. On a two-drawer filing cabinet, also of bleached wood, sat a surge protector, and half a dozen chargers ran like veins from the strip. Two different handheld video game units were still plugged in like small alien creatures on life support.

Justin turned on his computer system and stood back, offering Emma the chair. The system booted up in seconds, not the minutes it took her old computer. Before she'd even gotten the chair situated properly in front of the screen, the desktop display came to life.

A picture of a girl in a see-through blue bikini appeared on the screen. Emma blushed.

"Oh hey," Justin said, lunging over Emma's shoulder to grab the mouse. He slid it quickly over the desk and clicked. "Whoops."

A Web-browsing window soon filled the screen, blocking out the scantily clad model's picture. "Sorry," Justin said, pulling away.

"No problem," Emma said, also laughing now.

"Classy," Betina said.

"I think I'm going to get more coffee," he said. "You guys want anything?"

"I'm fine." Emma was already typing in the URL for the school's chat room.

"More coffee." Betina held her mug out toward Justin. "Black is fine."

"Like your clothes?"

"It's my signature color."

Justin took her mug. He walked quickly into the hallway.

"Emma's got a boyfriend," Betina sang quietly.

"Shut up. I do not."

"Well, you may have one before the day is over."

Though Emma protested, the idea sent a wave of excitement through her. It was totally wrong to even be thinking about something as lame as dating right now, but at the back of her mind, she wanted Betina to be right.

"Whatever. Come look at this."

Screen names filled McKinley High's chat room. Lines of text appeared quickly on the screen, only to be replaced a second later by more. Emma read as fast as she could, trying to catch up with the discussion.

. . . *floored him. It wasn't even a fight. Dickinson was full-on Jet Li. Barry didn't stand a chance.*

Barry deserved it. I was there.

Is anyone else hungry? Like really hungry? I've been starving since I got home.

Did u c Tess? OMG!!!!!

Tess was there? I thought she skipped.

She was there. Looked like a major skank.

She looked hot. Tess always looks
HAWT!

Nasty.

M serious. Like totally starving.

YOU STUPID ASSHOLES!! I'M
GOING TO KILL YOU DICK-
HEADS!!!

Whatevs, Clete.

KILL!

Someone's got his homicide on.

Barry sure did. . . .

"This is pointless," Betina said over Emma's shoulder. "They're just venting. They don't know anything."

"Maybe."

Emma typed: *Does anyone know*
what happened?

My dad said chemical spill.

drugs. really really good drugs.

global warming. we've made mother
earth sick and now she's fighting back.
keep it green.

KILL YOU ALL!

"See what I mean?"

Emma closed the chat window and opened a search
engine. She tried a number of different keyword

searches, but there seemed to be no news—nothing—about what had happened at her school. The only news she found was about the blizzard, and that wasn't good. Meteorologists expected a lull in the storm late afternoon, and then the blizzard was going to regroup and slam the mountain communities.

Justin returned to the room and handed Betina her coffee. He sipped from his own mug as he read over Emma's shoulder. "Crap. The storm isn't letting up."

"Not for a while," Emma agreed.

"Well, we're in good shape here if you guys have to stay. I think the Rover can get through a lot, but it's no snowplow. Let's see how things look after that guy from D.U. shows up."

Emma hated the idea of waiting around to see what might happen. She knew there was nothing else they could do, but it made her feel so helpless. So trapped.

14

Russ stared out the window at the milky haze of the blizzard. The ground and sky looked foggy, and in between snow pelted in violent blurs as if two clouds, one above and one below, were at war. The wind howled. A tree branch popped under the strain. Russ watched it crash into the snow covering his backyard.

He pictured Tess out in the violent weather. Her drawn, horrible face grinning at him through the haze, her black dress shredded and stained far worse than the last time he'd seen her. In his imagination, that's all he could picture: no body, no head, just her grin and her dress like the Cheshire cat gone rabid. For a split second she appeared there, next to the tree that had lost a limb. Her teeth. Her shredded clothes. Then a gust of snow erased the phantom.

"Topped off the crazy tank for one day," he said, and turned from the window.

The emptiness of the house was familiar, but today it settled on him like a scratchy shirt. Normally he saw his dad about ten minutes every day, and in the winter it could be days in between times they were actually in the same room together, but this emptiness was different; it was fabricated from the strange events of the last eighteen hours.

He kept thinking he should have asked for Emma's digits or address. He should have done something. If he had, he might not be alone in the house surrounded by a monster storm and cut off from everything.

But he hadn't, and now he'd have nothing to do all day except watch some TV and hang until his dad got home from work.

He thought about his father then and hoped he was okay. Red Foster worked damn hard, even though the doctor had told him to ease up. In the winter, he put in fourteen-hour days. One time Red had worked thirty-six hours straight behind the wheel of the snow-plow because the other two guys were out sick. His job title was City Maintenance Engineer, which was a fancy way of saying he was the town's handyman. In the winter, Red drove a snowplow and operated the tram system, which carried folks from the village over the ridge to the ski slopes. Usually he worked the graveyard shift on the plow from eleven at night until six in the morning, then he came home for some cof-fee and was at the tram controls in the Village

Promenade promptly at seven.

Russ didn't know how the old man managed, then reminded himself that his father wasn't that old. Red Foster was the same age as Vin Diesel. Russ had been stunned to learn this, because his dad looked so much older. Whereas the actor looked buff and youthful, Russ's father was heavy in the cheeks and neck with nests of wrinkles running from the puffy skin at his eyes.

Old or not, last year his father had been hospitalized with a "coronary incident." Even though Red wouldn't say the words, Russ knew his father had had a heart attack. The doctor told him to take it easy for a couple of weeks, but three days later, Red was back behind the wheel of the plow and at the controls of the tram.

Russ worried about his dad most days, and with a storm like this blowing down, he knew his hours on the plow could double.

As if Russ had conjured the man with his thoughts, the front door swung open, revealing his dad scraping his boots on the welcome mat. With the screen of gray-white behind him, Red Foster looked like a burly shadow. Wind howled through the open door, blowing the morning paper off the end table and scattering sheets over the couch.

"Born in a barn?" Russ said, joking around with his dad as he always did.

But his father wasn't in a joking mood.

"Shut the hell up," his dad growled.

The command took Russ off guard. His father had never been moody before and certainly never abusive, but an unfamiliar tone in his voice, its growling quality, told Russ something had changed.

"Sorry," he said quietly. His father stomped into the house and slammed the door. The man's face blazed red from the cold. He looked sallow and sick. "You okay?"

"Okay?" his dad asked. "When have I ever been okay? When has anything ever been okay?"

Russ didn't know how to respond, so he didn't. He backed out of the room. In the kitchen he poured a mug of coffee for his dad, intending to present it as a peace offering. Obviously, something major had happened. Maybe Red had gotten fired. A flare of fear went through Russ's chest as he thought about the possibility. It wasn't like his dad had mad skills. If he lost his job with the city, he wasn't likely to find another one.

Oh, crap, he thought. Would they have to move?

The kitchen door flew open, and his dad, looking even older and far angrier than Russ had ever seen him, loomed in the frame.

"You want some coffee?" Russ asked, holding up the mug.

"You want some coffee?" Red Foster mocked, his voice high-pitched and cruel. "I spend all night freezing my ass off in that plow and half a day punching buttons at the tram, and you can't even shovel the driveway? I gotta come home and do that too?"

"Hey," Russ said. He put the cup down. "I just got home like ten minutes ago. If you want me to shovel the drive, just ask. You don't have to be a tool about it."

"What did you call me?"

"I didn't call you anything. Look, what's wrong? Did something happen at work?"

"What did you call me!" his dad roared.

This was dangerous territory. Russ had never seen his dad behave this way, so angry and irrational. He didn't know how to defuse it. Panic trickled through his veins.

"I'm sorry," he tried, but his voice came out flat and insincere.

"You don't know the meaning of the word," his dad told him. "Sorry is marrying some stupid whore because she lied about using birth control and got knocked up. Sorry is having a kid before you're done growing up yourself. Sorry is having your wife take off with another man, leaving you with a brat you never wanted in the first place. Sorry is busting your ass day after day to feed that brat. Sorry is taking care of a worthless punk who ruined your life by being born."

His dad's words hit Russ in the chest like a series of punches. Disappointment and sadness and anger all vied for his attention as the bludgeoning words struck him. His eyes burned with the onset of tears, but Russ refused to cry. He didn't know what had happened to his dad today—maybe it was something really bad— but the old man had no right to take it out on him.

"Go to hell," Russ said. He waited for his dad to snap and yell more terrible words at him, but his dad said nothing. He just backed out of the kitchen and let the door swing closed.

Whatever, Russ thought. Great. Perfect. As if things weren't weird enough. Russ shook his head and pushed himself away from the counter. He looked back at the coffee mug sitting on the counter and felt an overwhelming urge to throw the thing against the wall, but he took a few deep breaths and the feeling passed.

He went to the phone and dialed Kit's number. When Kit answered, Russ said, "I'm coming over. Don't ask."

"I'm not even home, dude. I'm picking up my sisters."

"I'll meet you at your place."

"Uh . . . okay," Kit said.

Russ hung up and walked across the kitchen. He pushed open the door, and a blur of motion startled him. The edge of a snow shovel buried itself deep in the doorframe with a loud *thunk*! The handle blocked his exit like a turnstile bar.

"Jesus!" he cried, leaping back.

"I'll show you hell," his father yelled. "I'll send you there myself."

"What are you doing?" Russ cried.

The door swung closed, and Russ backed deeper into the kitchen. He looked around for another exit, knowing there wasn't one. The only openings in the kitchen were the door in front of him and a small window above the sink, but desperation confused him. Wood screeched, and Russ knew his father had pried the shovel's blade from the doorjamb. Red kicked open the door and stomped in.

"Tell *me* to go to hell? After everything I gave up . . .

for a kid I didn't even *want*?"

Russ didn't know what to do. His dad stood in front of the door holding the snow shovel tightly, his knuckles white, his fingers flushed with strain. If Russ tried to charge him, Red would cut him down before he got within three feet of the door. Despite his health problems, Russ's dad was strong.

"Why are you doing this?" Russ asked.

Instead of answering, Red glared at his son with hate-filled eyes. A low growling sound rose in his throat. Then he sprang forward, drawing the shovel back like an ax, ready to chop Russ down.

Russ ducked as the ridged green blade came for his head. It whispered through his hair, just missing a solid connection with his skull. Russ pivoted slightly and threw his body into his dad's, knocking him to the side. Red's boots must have still been wet from melting snow. They slipped and skidded on the kitchen floor. His feet went out from under him, sending the shovel flying into a cabinet. It clattered to the floor. Red made a final desperate attempt to right himself, but his balance was shot. He crashed back, hitting his head on the counter before collapsing to the floor.

Russ didn't stick around to see if his dad was badly injured. He could come to at any moment. *Or he could be dead.* Whatever the case, Russ fled.

Russ retrieved his jacket from the hook by the front door and left the house. He'd call the police from Kit's. Call an ambulance. He wanted his father to be okay, but Russ couldn't be certain the man lying on the kitchen floor was his father at all.

15

Sitting on the bed in his room, Justin watched Emma and Betina work at his keyboard. He was thinking about a girl he'd known in Houston. Her name was Laura, and one afternoon, Justin had offered her a ride home. Houston was under a storm warning because a nasty thunderstorm had perched over the city. Rain came down so heavy, it was like driving through a never-ending waterfall. But they'd made it back to his house, and he'd fixed them coffee and they'd spent the afternoon making out on the sofa in the media room while some lame Jim Carrey film played on the flat-panel. That had been an awesome afternoon, and it reminded him a little of today. If Betina hadn't come along for the ride, he might be getting to know Emma a lot better. That would have been cool. That would have been perfect. They had snow and a fire and plenty of beer left over from the party. They would have had the house to themselves with no chance of his parentals showing up. It would have been hot. Damn, it could have been an epic day.

Oh well, he thought. *Maybe next time.*

From Emma and Betina's conversation Justin gathered that news about the incident at McKinley High was slowly trickling onto the Web. The reports were vague, stating a student was hurt by a teacher. A photo taken by some kid with his cell phone showed two dozen students in front of the school hunched together and looking frightened amid the snowfall.

Justin left Emma and Betina in his room, scanning the internet. He walked to the living room and threw another log on the fire, which had nearly burned out. A single log fed a flickering yellow flame. They'd been in his room for hours, bouncing between the school chat and a variety of news sites. Betina called her mother frequently. Emma seemed obsessed with finding as much information as she could. Justin kept the coffeepot going. He wanted the bizarre crap to stop, wanted a fast return to normal.

After getting the fire stoked, he crossed to the wall of glass and peered into the gray gloom. The storm wasn't easing up the way the reports said it would. Not yet, anyway. He hadn't heard from the professor, who he imagined hadn't been able to make it through before the passes were closed. The guy surely would have called if he was in town.

Justin still hoped the man would show. Part of his disquiet about being in the house, a big part of it, had to do with that box. He had no idea what the thing was; he just knew it creeped him out.

Back in his bedroom, he found Emma and Betina sitting on the bed, talking.

"Did you give up?"

"Nothing new in the last half hour or so," Emma said. "They just keep repeating the info about what happened at school."

"And all of the cops and paramedics are tied up with the storm, so they couldn't be reached for comment," Betina added.

"Did you see anything about the storm letting up?" Justin asked.

"No," Emma said, sounding worried. "They say it's going to break for a while, then come back even stronger, but they don't say when. I hope Mom isn't trapped at the hotel all night."

"Well, you can stay here," Justin told her. Suddenly he realized that she might take his invitation as something a little more than friendly, and he blushed. "I mean, we have a guest room. If I can't get you guys home, I mean."

"We were just talking about that," Emma said.

"You could take us back to Betina's now and I could just crash at her place tonight, but that would leave you here alone."

"Yeah," Justin said, really hating that idea. "But if that's what you want, I'll be fine up here. I have everything I need."

"My place would be better," Betina said. "We don't have an altar to Sharper Image, but there's room enough."

"And it's closer to the village," Emma added. "We're kind of isolated out here, and if anything really bad happened, it could take an ambulance forever to reach us."

"What do you think is going to happen?" Justin wanted to know.

The doorbell interrupted Emma's reply. Emma's eyes lit up, and Betina whipped her head toward the sound.

"Must be the guy from D.U.," Justin said.

Emma and Betina clambered off the bed. Justin returned to the hall and followed it to the entryway. He looked through the glass beside the front door and saw a short, bald man with a thick white beard. The man wore a black overcoat with a gray fur collar. The coat, the collar, and the man's head were liberally salted with snow.

"Is it him?" Emma asked.

"It's either him or Santa Claus," Justin replied. "How did he make it through the storm? The road has been closed for hours."

"He might have reached the village this morning and was just waiting for you to get home from school."

"Hello," the man called. Justin checked the window again, and the bearded face was pressed against the glass. "I'm Ernest Banks, from Denver University. We had an appointment? I know I'm early, but the storm . . ."

"Sure," Justin replied, reaching out to unlock the door. "Just a sec."

As soon as the door was opened, the man scurried into the entryway, causing all three of them to back up a step. He wiped frantically at his head and slapped at the lapels of his long coat, sending a shower of white flakes to the tiled floor.

"Sorry. Sorry. Sorry," Banks said. He continued slapping himself, clearing away the remaining bits of snow. He talked fast, words running together in a rapid-fire delivery. "I'm frozen to the bone, to the bone. My car got stuck at the bottom of the hill. First they close the passes, then I almost get buried in an avalanche, which

I imagine is going to shut things down for a while, and I'd better consider finding a place to stay for the night. Can you recommend a hotel?" He didn't wait for anyone to reply. "Frozen. Just frozen. I make it through all of that and then I get stopped at the bottom of this here drive by a few feet of snow. Can you imagine? So, I walked. Of course I walked. I can't fly. Ridiculous thing to say, but it's quite a walk up that drive, and I am absolutely frozen through."

Justin didn't know if the man was finished or if he was just pausing for breath. He looked on, amused, realizing that suddenly no one was saying anything.

"There's a fire," Emma finally said. "Why don't you go warm up? Justin, is there any coffee left?"

"What? Oh yeah, should be. Would you like some coffee?"

"Coffee," Banks said as if Justin were offering him gold. "Hot and black, please. Now, where's that fire? Oh, there it is. Wonderful." He charged toward the living room, all but oblivious to the others. "I've seen the oddest things today. Quite a colorful little village you have. I imagine people get themselves all worked up when a storm comes in, but I have to say, it was looking rather primitive down there. Yes, 'primitive' is the right word. People bickering over loaves of bread and ice-cream bars. Can you imagine wanting an ice-cream bar in this weather? I certainly can't. Ridiculous, but as I said, I imagine this kind of storm makes people skittish. It triggers something in the reptile part of the brain—you know, survival instincts and whatnot."

Banks leaned close to the fire and scrubbed his hands together. Justin headed for the kitchen to get the hyper old guy some coffee. When he returned, Banks was still by the fire, still scrubbing his hands and still talking.

"Met the oddest young woman down there. Well, *met* is a rather strong word. She was standing in the middle of the road and I stopped to ask if she needed anything, and she just smiled—it was a dreadful little grin—and she said she already had what she needed, and I drove on. Poor girl. She really has taken the whole dieting thing too far. Thank you," Banks gushed, accepting the coffee from Justin. He held it close to his beard with both hands, letting the steam warm his face.

Justin noticed that both Emma and Betina seemed amused by the professor's endless chattering. Looking at the professor, he saw something like worry flash across Banks's face. Banks put the coffee to his lips and sipped, but he peered over the edge of the mug. His eyes danced from Justin to Emma to Betina and back again.

Like he's sizing us up, Justin thought.

"So!" Banks announced. "I understand you have something for me. Something quite interesting. I must say I was a little disappointed when I first saw the photograph of the piece. Hardly looked interesting at all, just a rather plain little cube, but I will admit that the method of its discovery interested me greatly. I'd like to think it has some relevance, but more than likely it's just a child's toy, maybe worth a few hundred dollars on eBay for the right collector but hardly an important find."

"It's not a toy," Betina said, "unless it's for a seriously twisted kid."

"You didn't open it, did you?" Banks asked, worry clouding his features. His eyes narrowed as he again looked from face to face.

"No," Justin lied.

Banks must have read the deceit on his face.

"Oh my, oh my, oh my," Banks whispered, shaking his head slowly.

"What?" Emma asked. "Do you know what it is?"

"What I know is my business," Banks snapped. He

turned to Justin. "I left very clear instructions with your father that no one was to open the box. No one!"

"Hey, man," Justin said, "it just happened, and I didn't do it, so lighten up."

"Lighten up?" Banks launched his mug against the mantel, splashing coffee across the wall. The cup shattered, and bits of ceramic tinkled to the stone hearth. "It was mine," the professor shouted. "Mine! You had no right to open that box. You shouldn't have even been allowed to touch something so precious."

"Okay, freak," Justin said, his voice trembling, "you need to leave, like now."

"What is it?" Emma asked. "We didn't open it, but it was opened, and I think something bad is happening because of it."

"It was mine!" Banks said, ignoring Emma's plea. The old man stomped his feet like a troll from a story. "I couldn't believe people like you had found it. You didn't deserve it. You didn't *earn* it."

"Out," Justin said. He'd had more than enough of the crazy old jerk. It was bad enough that news of the party was likely to get back to his dad. He wasn't going to let this old guy trash the house. Besides, he could turn violent. Justin reached out to grab Banks, but the old man sprang away quickly.

"And now you've opened it. Well, I guess you deserve it. You deserve all the misery fate can rain down on you, but I want that box."

"Get out of my house," Justin yelled. He crossed to the fireplace and retrieved the iron poker from the rack. He brandished it before him like a sword, sending Banks stumbling backward.

"Give me what I came for," Banks yelled back. "Give me what is mine."

"I'll give you a cracked skull," Justin replied. He lunged forward, and Banks darted to the side, putting the sofa between himself and Justin.

Betina and Emma ran for the front door. Betina yanked it open and screamed, "Get out of here!"

"Get out," Emma echoed, apparently no longer concerned with what Banks knew about the box.

Banks turned his head from side to side, eyeing first Justin, then the girls by the front door. His head moved fast, like a terrier receiving commands from two masters.

Justin ran around the side of the sofa and took a swing at the professor. The point of the poker grazed the shoulder of the man's coat. Banks yelped and took off running for the door.

"It's mine," Banks shouted.

Justin poured on the steam and was almost within striking distance of the professor when Banks leaped outside, falling forward to land in the snow accumulating on the walk. Emma flung herself at the door and slammed it closed, pressing her body against it as she fumbled with the locks.

"What the hell?" Justin said.

A weight of tension fell from his neck and shoulders. He was still breathing heavily from the confrontation, but his mind told him the immediate threat was over and anxiety rolled off of him in great waves. It left him light-headed, though his body was still stoked with adrenaline.

"Are you okay?" Emma asked, looking at him with such warmth, he couldn't help but smile.

"Fine," he said. "Just glad it's over."

"Mine!"

Wham!

Banks hit the outside of the door so hard, Justin imagined he could feel the blow from several feet away. Emma spun from the door and rejoined Betina against the wall.

"I don't think it's over yet," Emma said.

16

Emma backed away from the door. Both Betina and Justin looked just as worried as she felt. Outside, Banks pounded on the door with such fury, the jamb rattled.

"That idiot is going to break his hands," Justin said.

Emma knew Justin was right. How could Banks keep hitting the door so savagely? He had to be hurting himself.

"I'm calling the cops," Justin said. He fished his cell phone from the pocket of his jeans and tried punching the buttons, but he still held the fire poker in his other hand and it was swaying clumsily in his grip. "Here," he said, handing the poker to Emma.

She took the heavy piece of iron, wrapping her fingers around its handle tightly. Behind her, glass shattered, and she whipped around to see one of Banks's hands slapping the inside of the door, seeking the locks. Blood dripped from his mangled hand and smeared the interior of the door where he touched it.

"Do something," Betina said.

Emma swung the poker at the hand. It was a tentative strike, weak and ineffective. Despite the situation, she hated the idea of hurting anyone.

Banks's fingers found the chain lock and began jiggling the fastener in the track. Emma took another swing and this time she put some force behind it.

Banks howled. His hand slithered back through the window like a startled snake. Emma kept her eyes on the gap in the glass. The line of blood along the jagged edge made her queasy, but she refused to look away. Outside, Banks continued to cry, occasionally screaming, "Mine. It's mine."

"I'm on hold," Justin announced, waving his cell phone in the air.

"Well, what are we supposed to do?" Emma asked.

"Keep doing what you're doing," Betina said. "Beat Santa's ass."

The noises of Banks's complaints faded, and Emma felt a moment of relief. Maybe the old man had had enough and was retreating. Once the sounds were little more than whispers amid the crying wind, she leaned over and checked the window beside the door.

Banks was gone. She squinted into the storm to see if she could make out his shape farther down the driveway, but the weather was too frantic for her to see anything except the nose of Justin's Range Rover, and even that was blurred and shadowed by the snowfall. Still, the professor was nowhere in sight. Emma breathed deeply and turned away. Her knees felt weak, and she leaned against the door for support. She looked at Betina, who continued to gnaw on her thumbnail, and at Justin, who looked annoyed, his cell pressed against his head.

"Is he gone?" Justin asked.

"I think so. I hit him pretty hard."

"He could have gone around the side of the house," Betina noted.

"Nothing over there but the garage," Justin replied. "He couldn't get the door open and even if he did, the kitchen door is locked. We'd hear him long before he got in."

"What about the other side of the house?" Emma asked.

"Same thing. Even if he smashed a window, we'd be able to reach the room before he hauled his fat ass in."

"You're sure all the doors are locked?"

"Yeah," he said. "I checked earlier while you guys were on the computer. The only other door to the outside is the one off the kitchen." Justin turned to indicate it with a wave, but he didn't complete the gesture.

Emma saw why. Beyond the living room windows, a dark form pushed through the snowfall like a thick, squat shadow.

Banks stepped into view as if passing through a gray curtain. His left hand hung uselessly at his side, but his right arm was cocked back.

"Oh, crap," Justin said. "Don't!"

Banks whipped his arm forward, sending a fist-sized rock flying at the window. The stone punched a hole in the glass and hit the rug a foot short of the coffee table. Banks grinned broadly, but the expression melted into a vicious sneer. He waded through the calf-high snow, pushing low ridges across the surface as he went.

None of them moved. Emma wanted to. She knew she should be running toward the window to cut off Banks before he smashed his way into the house, but she was frozen in place.

"It's mine!" Banks bellowed through the hole in the glass.

"Give me that," Justin said, yanking the poker out of Emma's hand. He handed her the cell phone, and she placed it to her ear but heard nothing on the other end except hissing. "He thinks he's going to come into my house and tear things up? I'm taking his ass down."

But Justin didn't even get two steps before a second figure appeared beyond the glass. Doug Nichols emerged from the storm and flew at Banks. He hit the man at the waist and tackled him, forcing Banks's head beneath the snow. Doug pulled his arm back and delivered three fast and powerful punches to the man's face. More shadows formed in the storm. The black smudges lightened and took shape: At least ten more students were walking toward Justin's house. They pushed forward, becoming distinct like frozen corpses floating to the surface of an icy lake. Emma didn't know all of the students, but they looked wrong together. Geeks and Cools and Sweats gathered around Doug; then they descended on the beaten old man. Brian Knott from the basketball team stomped his foot into the trench of snow where Banks lay. Clete Morrisey knelt down and punched violently. Laney Hoffman kicked, and Laurent Miller jabbed the body with a long stick. One of Banks's hands swatted at the air in a vain attempt to hold off his attackers. Clete grabbed the man's wrist and bit deeply into his hand. Banks screamed. The sound was horrible.

"They're going to kill him," Justin whispered in disbelief.

Emma knew he was right.

Banks's screams stopped abruptly. Certainly he must have been beaten unconscious, but the students continued the assault. Blood speckled the snow beyond the window. A rivulet of crimson dripped down the glass.

"This is crazy!" Betina screamed. "What's wrong with you people?"

Doug stood from the attack on Banks and turned to face them through the glass. His face looked too thin, and his eyes blazed with derangement. He walked to the hole in the window.

"Where's the box?" he asked, his voice gravelly and tinged with sick amusement. "Give it to me and we won't have to juice you the way we did Grandpa."

The other students continued their attack on Banks. Their hands and shoes were bathed in red, but they didn't stop.

Emma's throat tightened in disgust. She couldn't look any longer. She took the cell phone from her ear and put it in her pocket. Help wasn't coming. No one was coming. They were alone, miles from town, with a dozen insane kids ripping an old man apart in the backyard.

Once they finish with Banks, they'll probably do the same to us, she thought. *The only reason they're still hitting Banks is because they're enjoying it. They're having fun.*

"The box?" Doug asked. "We're just about done out here. You wouldn't want us to come in there."

"I'd better get it," Justin said. His voice sounded dull and hollow in her ears.

"What?" Emma asked. "Wait, you're just going to give it to them?"

"We don't have any choice. We don't even know what it is, and I'm not willing to die for it."

"Look," she said, grabbing Justin's arm, "I'll get it. I'd feel safer knowing you're keeping an eye on them." She nodded at the window.

Justin looked nervous. Still, he agreed. "It's in my dad's office. Third door down on the right. It's on his desk."

"Okay," Emma said, anxious nerves making her feel sick. "Just give me a minute."

She entered the hall determined to retrieve the box and hand it over to Doug Nichols. Maybe it was foolish, simply a response to excessive menace and underused confidence, but she didn't care. She'd been through enough for one day—they all had. If handing over the damn box would make the nightmare end, so be it. The thing had already been opened, and she no longer questioned its responsibility for the madness that followed, so what difference did it make? The damage was done.

So why do they want it? she wondered. *Why was Banks so desperate to possess the box? Why was Doug?*

Because the damage isn't *done,* she thought. *It's just getting started. Doug wants the box so he can open it again. He wants to release a second swarm and afflict more people. Who knows how many people he intends to infect?*

The certainty crystallized in her mind.

"No," she whispered, walking into the office. "They can't have it."

The box sat on top of the desk. She grabbed it and winced at its strange, fleshy texture. Quickly, she left the office and crossed the hall to Justin's bedroom. She lifted his book bag from the floor. She unzipped the large compartment and dumped the contents on the floor and shoved the box inside. Justin's keys, including the keys to the Range Rover, sat on the desk next to his computer keyboard. She snagged them and turned away from the desk. With the bag secured over her shoulders, she remembered Justin's cell phone in her pocket. She called Betina's number and prayed she would answer.

As the phone rang, Emma went to the window and slid it open. She was already climbing out when Betina answered.

"Yeah?" Betina said, sounding nervous.

"It's Emma," she whispered, lifting one foot onto the windowsill. "Pretend I'm someone else."

"I know, Mom," Betina answered.

Good. She's playing along.

"Get Justin and run. I've got the keys to his car. Run out the front door and meet me at his car. I'm climbing out his window now. We can't let them get the box."

"Okay, Mom," Betina said, pouring on the sarcasm for effect. "I'll be sure to wear my scarf."

The muffled sound of glass shattering came through one ear as a much clearer crashing came over the phone. Betina screeched and Justin shouted. Emma leaped from the window and landed in deep snow. She ran for the Range Rover, keys jangling in her hands. As she crossed the front of the house, she looked at the front door.

It flew open, and Emma kept running.

17

Justin held the fireplace poker tightly, never taking his eyes off Doug. The others had finished with Banks as soon as Emma disappeared into the hallway. He was glad she'd decided to give up the box. It wasn't like any of them knew what to do with it—or even knew what it was. Besides, even if they had wanted to keep it, there was no way the three of them could take on all of those lunatics outside. He looked at them and felt ill.

The crazy teens formed a tight semicircle behind Doug. They stood motionless, like perverse statues. All of them shared a sickly, drawn look and manic eyes. Blood dripped from their fingers and stained their clothes.

"She really should hurry," Doug said. "I can't imagine this window slowing us down much."

"She just left," Justin said.

"Maybe we should come inside," Doug taunted.

"No," Justin said. "I'm in enough trouble because of that window."

"Do you really think that's your biggest problem right now?" Doug asked, smiling dangerously. He looked at the remains of Ernest Banks. Snow frosted the motionless body. Blood melted the accumulation in sporadic patches, and steam rose from the fresh wounds.

"Just give her a second."

"Maybe we should just come inside," Doug repeated. "You're being a terrible host, making us wait out here in the cold."

Beside him a phone rang. Justin backed up a step, thinking the noise would trigger an attack from Doug, but the boy remained in the snow, staring in at them.

"I know, Mom," Betina said. Justin looked at her. She was rolling her eyes and shaking her head as if thoroughly annoyed by the call. "Okay, Mom. I'll be sure to wear my scarf."

Before Betina could finish the last word, the living room window exploded inward. Betina shrieked and Justin cried out. He spun around to see Doug stepping out of the snow and climbing into the living room.

"Time's up," he said. "I guess we gotta get sticky again."

The crazies poured through the window. A hand

on Justin's arm tugged him backward, and he saw that it was Betina.

"Come on," she said.

"Emma?" he replied.

"She's outside."

Justin spun around, needing no further encouragement. He unfastened the locks in three quick motions and threw the door open. Ushering Betina over the threshold, he saw Emma loping through the snow, moving with surprising agility toward his car.

"Run," Betina shouted, not looking back.

Justin did just that. He tore off along the walk beneath the eaves of the house, where the snow was only piled up to the tops of his shoes. At the drive he veered to the right and met Emma at the driver's side door of his SUV. She held out the keys to him, but they wouldn't do any good. From where he stood he could see the back tire.

It had been slashed. Considering the Rover wasn't tipping, both of the back tires must have been cut.

He looked back and was surprised to find that Doug and his mob of lunatic kids hadn't followed them out to the front of the house yet.

They know we aren't going anywhere, Justin thought. *They don't have any reason to hurry.*

"What are you waiting for?" Emma asked.

"The tires," Justin said. He waited for her to see the damage for herself.

Emma looked and turned back to him. She was furious.

"Then we run," she said. "They are not getting this box."

"Run? Are you nuts?"

Emma didn't reply. Instead, she turned and began wading through the snow, making her way toward the end of the drive. Betina set off after her friend.

Justin had no choice but to follow.

18

Russ Foster hung up Kit's phone and fell back on his friend's bed. He'd never gotten through to an emergency operator, and concern for his dad burned his chest. He thought about the man lying on the kitchen floor bleeding, possibly dead, and it made him sick, but he didn't want to go back to the house. His unease had grown more pronounced while he'd assisted Kit with his chores, which included shoveling the driveway and sidewalks in front of the house.

"I gotta do that too?" his father had raged.

Now they were kicking back, alone in the house. Kit's mother had come home from work and gathered up the girls for a last-minute hoarding spree at the supermarket.

"Still no answer?"

"Nope. The line is still busy. *Please hold.*" The last two words came out as a frustrated whisper. Russ looked at the ceiling, noticing the light fixture. It was glass, with vines and leaves etched into the dome. He'd been in Kit's room a thousand times and never noticed it before. "What the hell is going on out there?"

"The end of days," Kit said. He actually sounded excited about the prospect. "It's like the apocalypse or something."

"Don't be stupid," Russ replied. "A few people freaking out is hardly a sign of the end of the world."

"Yeah, well, how do you think it happens? You think someone's going to send out an email to everyone that says, 'Dude, time's up,' and then launch the nukes? No way. It starts small, like a cancer or something, and then it spreads."

"You're nuts."

"Why am I nuts? Why does everyone think it's going to be some totally rational thing that comes along and wipes us out? Viruses? Wars? A meteor? Global warming? What if we just reach a point, like some biological finish line, and we freak out and start offing each other? What if it's like coded into our genes, like Mother Nature's fail-safe when things get out of control?"

"Are you serious?" Russ shook his head, now gazing at the faint shadows of vines and leaves the light fixture cast on the ceiling.

Kit was always going on about one conspiracy or

another. Sometimes it was funny, and sometimes it was interesting, but with all the weirdness in the air, Russ now found it nothing but annoying. He should have tried to change the subject, but what could he change it to? You didn't see everything you knew go crazy and then kick back and discuss the weather.

"I'm totally serious. Like last night at the party. What the hell was that? Someone opens a box and all of this glitter crap goes airborne? It's like out of a fairy tale, but you saw it and I saw it."

"And more than likely, whatever that crap was is causing this."

"No way," Kit said. He stood from his chair and crossed to the bed. He leaned over into Russ's field of vision. "You and me are fine and we were right there. Vic Hoffman wasn't. And that old couple fighting in the street? What about them? They so weren't on the guest list. No way. Nowhere near Moore's house. And what about your dad?"

"Don't even," Russ warned. He didn't want to get into that.

"Fine. Okay. Whatever. I'm just saying, this is affecting people who weren't there and is not affecting people who were. It's like humankind has hit the finish line."

"Quit saying that."

"Right, well, you just keep thinking we're okay until a meteor hits Earth or the ice caps melt, but I'm telling you we'll be our own extinction event."

"Where do you get this crap?"

"I'm just saying—"

"Well, quit *saying* until you have something intelligent to say."

"Dude, wait and see."

"Right."

"You won't have to wait long."

"Fine," Russ said. He sat up on the bed and reached for the phone again.

He put the receiver to his ear, but there was no dial tone. The lines were down. He held up the receiver and rocked it in the air. Kit looked at it like a kitten eyeing a ball of string.

"It's dead," Russ told him.

19

Finally, they stopped to rest. Emma felt like she'd been running for an hour, but it had been only a handful of minutes. Initially, they had stuck to the drive and the road, but they'd heard the calls of the freaked teens behind them and a truck's engine. She had known the road wasn't safe, and they'd bolted into the trees at the bottom of the drive, stomping a makeshift trail through the woods. Pine trees blocked some of the storm's fury, but it was darker here. Snow swirled in the air against a backdrop of black space and gray bark.

The road had made running difficult. The woods made it nearly impossible. Emma could barely push through the snow-choked brush. Betina trudged next to her, uncharacteristically quiet. Justin moved with remarkable grace through the obstructions, but he paused frequently, checking over his shoulder for Doug and the others. They weren't far behind. Voices rose up. Sometimes it was only the wind, creating meaningless noise that just sounded like words. Other times, Emma had no doubt their pursuers were very nearby.

Trembling with cold, Emma sat on a fallen log. Betina joined her, but Justin kept pacing in the snow before them. None of them had coats or gloves or hats. There hadn't been time to gather these necessities.

"We need to think about this," Justin said, leaning close to her ear so he didn't have to shout over the gusting wind. His teeth chattered. Everyone's teeth chattered. "We could get lost in this, and we'll freeze in an hour if we don't find some shelter."

"Do you know any of your neighbors?" Emma asked.

"Doesn't matter if we know them," he said. "If we can get to a house, they'll let us in."

"Unless they're as whacked-out as Doug and his buddies," Betina said.

"Yeah," Justin agreed.

Emma could tell by the way his face fell that Justin hadn't thought of that. She didn't blame him. The cold and the storm and the panic made it tough to think straight.

"Okay," he continued, "we've already passed the Ensons' place and the Yarborough house. We can't go back. Doug and the others must be following our tracks, so we have to keep moving forward. If we're where I think we are, we need to head that way." He pointed to the left. Then his face lit up. "Yeah, okay. Come on."

Emma raised herself from the log. Her cheeks and forehead felt like someone was pressing a frozen steel plate to them. She could barely feel her fingers.

"Where are we going?" Emma asked.

"There's a cabin," Justin said. "I don't know who owns the place, but a lot of the cabins out here are seasonal. Guys in the city keep them for skiing week-ends. It could be empty if the owner didn't make it through before the passes were closed."

"Or some knife-wielding psycho is waiting for us there." Betina wasn't joking. Emma could tell this was a serious concern for her.

"Would you rather freeze to death?" Justin asked.

"How did my life come down to these two options?"

"Betina," Emma said, putting her hand on her friend's shoulder, "we have to keep moving. If nothing else, the exercise will keep us warm."

"Nothing is going to make me feel warm. I'll never feel warm again, but let's go. I know you're right."

They continued through the thickening gloom. Night was coming. If they got trapped in the woods after full dark, they'd never find their way out. Emma knew it. They had to keep moving, and if the cabin didn't work out, they needed to head downhill. Eventually they'd reach the village. Someone would help them if they reached the village. They just had to.

Distantly, she heard something that might have been a truck's engine. She couldn't be sure.

It'll be okay, she told herself. *The snow is so thick, I can't see twenty feet. It'll be harder for them to spot us.*

But they can follow our tracks. The grooves in the snow are so deep, we'd never be able to hide them. All they have to do is pick up the trail and follow it to us.

Her ears and nose stung. The cold tremors increased until they became a persistent quaking throughout her body. She thought she might shake apart at any moment.

Where is this damn cabin?

Emma looked up and saw a swirling gray-white cloud ahead of them. Snow whirled thickly, but the atmosphere carried more light. They were emerging from the woods. She and Betina followed Justin out to the center of a wide patch of cleared snow. Justin stepped to the right and suddenly vanished as if he'd dropped through a hole in the earth. Emma ran forward, calling his name, and saw the ground cut away beneath her, becoming a dramatic downhill slope. Below her a dark blur hurtled through the storm. Justin? Then the snow gave out under her shoes.

She fell onto her backside, her legs splaying out ahead of her. A moment later, gravity grabbed her firmly and yanked her down the slope. She dropped back. The edge of the box ground into her spine, and Emma felt a sharp dread that it might break or open as she skidded down the hill. Wind rushed past her at a frightening speed. The sensation of her stomach dropping out, an overpoweringly nasty sensation she associated with flying in airplanes, punched her in the midsection. She slid blind to what lay ahead, throwing her hands out in the hopes of finding something to hold on to or at least something to slow her down, but her momentum increased. The snow pack rose up beneath her, and she rocketed into the air. A moment later, she hit the thick powder and started to roll. She cried out, everything turning and smearing from white to gray to white again. Then something soft embraced her, slowed her, stopped her.

It felt as if she'd passed out for a second. One

moment she was tumbling down the slope uncontrollably, then she was cradled in a vast snowbank at the bottom of the hill. Her confusion passed so quickly. It seemed her mind had erased the terrible flipping at the end of the run. She was sliding. Then she was safe.

Emma dug her way out of the bank in time to see Betina rolling out of the storm toward her. She got to the side just in time and watched her friend roll into the dent Emma's body had left in the snowbank. Quickly, she reached into the book bag and pulled the box free, grateful to see it remained undamaged and unopened. Emma carefully returned the thing to the bag and slung it over her shoulder before checking out their surroundings.

Ahead of them stood a small cabin. No lights burned from the building, but Emma's heart lightened to see the place. Shelter. Warmth.

Too bad we can't stay here, she thought.

"So are we safe?" Betina asked, brushing powder from her chest.

"Doubtful," Emma replied, speaking loudly to be heard over the wind. "If those guys really want that box, they'll keep hunting us, and I figure they've lived here long enough to know every house on this mountainside. If they're following our tracks, they'll be all over us in a few minutes."

"We should still check the place out," Justin said. "There might be guns or something inside. If nothing else, they might have warm clothes."

"We can look," Emma said uncertainly.

They worked through the snow to the cabin. Once they were on the porch, Emma brushed off her clothes and stomped the snow from her boots. She looked at the front windows and figured the place was empty. She wasn't sure if that was good news or not. Of course, if the door was locked and nobody was home, they'd be out of luck.

Or not.

Justin didn't even try the doorknob before jamming the fireplace poker through the door's window. A second later, he shoved his hand through the opening and unlocked the door.

"Hey," Emma said. "That's . . ." *Illegal.*

"Desperate times call for desperate measures," Justin said with a small grin. He swung the door open and held it for them. "Come on. It isn't getting any warmer out here."

So they entered the cabin. It was small and neatly kept, with simple wooden furniture and exposed beams above. Emma knew immediately they couldn't stay here. Large windows opened along three walls. No way to secure the place against an attack. They needed to gather what they could and leave.

So now I'm a thief, Emma thought.

"Check the closets and the kitchen," Justin said. "Look for anything you can use as a weapon or to keep warm."

They scavenged the rooms thoroughly. Betina found several pairs of gloves and scarves for the three of them in a chest of drawers. She took a knife from the kitchen and brandished it in Emma's face.

"Don't I look all dangerous?"

"You look cold. Check the living room closet for a coat."

Emma crossed to the phone affixed to the kitchen wall. No dial tone. Great. She leaned back on the counter and took a deep breath. Justin walked in a second later wearing the gloves Betina had given him and a really silly-looking red scarf.

"You okay?" he asked.

"I guess. I mean, considering everything . . . I'm doing pretty good."

"Yeah, good." He leaned on the counter next to her and put his hand on the book bag. "Why didn't you just give it to them?"

"Because Tess wants it."

"Tess?" he asked. "I didn't see her wasting that professor back at my place."

"I know, but I've been thinking about this. The way she looked this morning, the way she acted; it just feels like she's the key. I mean, Doug and Barry left with her last night after she fainted, right? Both of them went crazy today. That guy from the university, Banks, said he saw a really skinny girl when he was driving in, and you saw what happened to him. Remember what she said in the teachers' lounge? Something about her vessel? She has to mean the box. I think she sent Doug out to get it."

"Then let's hide it. Sure, they might tear this place apart looking, but we could bury it in the snow somewhere and come back when this is over."

"What if something happens to us?" Emma challenged. "Someone will just find it and open it again. We have to get to someone in charge, and we have to let them know exactly what's happening."

As Emma spoke, Betina returned to the kitchen wearing a parka four sizes too large for her. She punched at her cell phone, held the device to her ear, and shook her head.

"Nine-one-one is still out," Betina said.

"Well, we can't just wait here," Emma said. "We need to find help."

"There are a couple more coats in the closet. They're huge, though. The guy who lives here must be a professional wrestler or something."

"As long as they're warm."

The three left the kitchen, and Emma headed for the closet. Betina had been right, the coats were big; they looked like sleeping bags dangling from the hangers. On the shelf above the clothing bar, Emma found a Maglite with a long metal barrel. She knew it was getting dark outside. Night was coming on fast. They might need it. She pulled the flashlight off the shelf and thumbed it on. The beam cut neatly through the gloom of the closet.

She handed the light to Justin while she pulled on a massive white ski parka with sleeves nearly a foot longer than her arms. She rolled them up the best she could and retrieved the light from Justin.

"Grab a coat and let's go," she said, already heading for the front door.

They left the cabin just in time. When she stepped out onto the porch, she heard shouts coming from up the hill. It wouldn't be long before Doug and the others discovered the sledding path—not long at all before they descended on the cabin.

She slogged through the snow in the general direction of the road. She couldn't be certain they were going the right way because the air was frantic with snowflakes and it was getting dark, but based on the position of the house, she thought they were going in the right direction. Betina moved up to her side, holding the knife far from her body like something that stinks.

When they reached the road, Emma glanced back toward the house. Doug and the others were coming. They moved in a pack over the field of snow, looking like a single, giant-shadowed beast, undulating and slithering over the ground toward them.

20

· *This sucks*, Justin thought.

Feet freezing, nose running from the cold, cheeks and chin tingling with sharp needles of pain, Justin trudged down the road. Already, drifting snow had made the street impossible to navigate for vehicles, except for plows and snowmobiles. Emma moved steadily at his side. She looked strong and determined, her eyes squinting to see the road ahead. Betina slogged on next to her.

Once this was over he was going home and grabbing a bottle of his dad's best whiskey and curling up in front of the television. He never wanted to be cold again, never wanted to see another snowflake.

"What is that?" Emma asked, pointing ahead.

Justin followed her gloved finger and saw two small lights piercing the blizzard. His heart skipped a beat as worry came and went. At first, he'd thought the lights belonged to Doug's truck, but they were too high and too small. Like yellow eyes, they gazed through the frantic storm.

They came upon the snowplow five minutes later. Betina yelped with joy, seeing the giant machine nestled behind a bank of snow. Emma smiled, and it was a beautiful sight.

But Justin remained cautious in his optimism. As they approached the motionless vehicle, he noticed the windshield wore a blanket of white. The front lights were off, though the fog lights on the roof of the machine still burned. Carefully, Justin worked his way over the drift to the side of the plow. The road behind it was still covered in snow, but it was a minor accumulation compared to what they'd been walking through. Maybe two inches deep.

Of course, he didn't want to walk. His hope was that the driver of the plow would taxi them down to the village, or at least call someone to pick them up.

Justin climbed the side of the plow and tried the door, but it was locked. He wiped away powder from the glass and was surprised to see a man sitting behind the wheel. His shoulders slumped, and his head cocked to the side. In the dim light, it looked like he was napping. Justin rapped on the window and was grateful to see the man move, one thick arm reaching for the door. But it didn't open. The man's arm withdrew and returned to his side.

Justin tried the door and it opened.

"Are you okay?" Justin asked.

"What's going on?" Emma called from the street.

"I don't know," he replied. He turned his attention back to the man.

He was an old guy with a big gut. His soft cheeks sagged over his jaw like the flaps of a hound's muzzle. The old guy appeared dazed, maybe wounded.

"Are you okay?" Justin repeated, raising his voice to be heard over the wind.

"Just fine," the plow driver said. "Fine as frog's hair."

"Are you hurt?"

"Nah'p. Just relaxing a bit. Feels nice to relax, good to do nothing at all."

"We need your help," Justin said. "Some people are chasing us and we have to get down to the village."

"Village is back that way," the driver said, slowly moving his head to indicate the relatively cleared path behind the plow.

"I know where the village is," Justin said. "Can you take us down there?"

"Nah'p. I'm fine right here."

"Look, this is serious. They want to kill us."

"Sounds like a lot of work."

Infuriated with the driver, Justin lunged into the cab and grabbed the man by his jacket. He gave him a good shake, but the man continued to look sleepy and uninterested.

"You have got to get us out of here."

"Nah'p."

Emma appeared beside him. She leaned against him as she got her balance on the running board of the plow.

"What's wrong?"

"I don't know," Justin said. "This guy is out of it. Probably high or something."

"Just relaxing," the driver interjected.

"Let me try," Emma said. "Mister, I'm sorry we're bothering you, but it's really important that you get us down to the village. We're in a lot of trouble and really scared."

The plow driver smiled lightly and leaned his head back on the seat. "What you need is a good nap. Once you get some rest, you'll feel a lot better."

"I'm sure you're right, but we can't rest until we get to town. Please, if you'd just give us a ride?"

"Nah'p. Need to rest. It's dangerous to operate this here machine if you aren't rested."

"Then could you please call someone and let them

know where we are?"

Muffled voices rose up from the storm. Justin barely heard them, and if he weren't so keyed up, he might have thought they were nothing more than wind song blowing through tree branches. Then a shrill call sliced the air, and he knew the pack of students was getting close.

"Mister?" Emma insisted. "Mister, if you'd just call someone."

"We have to go," Justin told her, taking her sleeve in a gloved hand. "He's useless, and he's too big to move. I can't drive this thing sitting on his lap. I won't fit."

"But we can't stay out in this storm," Emma protested.

"And if we wait here, Doug and the others are going to catch us. Can't you hear that?"

The cries in the storm grew louder, more furious. The shouts melted into the wind and bounced off the thick padding of snow, making the words sound like a distant chant heard through several walls.

Justin gave the plow driver a final look. The man's head was again cocked to the side. His lips were turned up in a gentle smile, as if he was in the middle of a pleasant dream. Emma finally gave up and leaped down to the snow-covered road. Justin slammed the plow door and followed.

Three minutes later, they took the bend in the road and headed down a steep slope. Behind them, the lunatic posse attacked the snowplow.

Justin couldn't wait to get down to the village, to safety and the company of normal people. They'd hand the box over to the cops and be done with the whole thing. Then he was going to pretend this day had never happened.

21

"Lock the back door!" Kit Urban yelled.

Russ didn't ask questions but ran as fast as he could through the kitchen. He skidded to a stop by the door and cranked the lock just as a gaunt face floated into view beyond the glass. It was a woman with stringy brown hair. Her mouth was smeared with a greasy paste, and bits of food clung to it. She snarled at him and punched her hand through the window before Russ could back away. Her fingers clawed at his coat, trying to get a grip on him. Russ turned and struck out with his hand, knocking the woman's arm to the side. A shard of glass cut her elbow, but she didn't even seem to notice.

"I'm hungry," she cried. "So hungry. You have to give me something to eat."

Russ didn't reply. He backed away and ran into Kit.

"Dude, we're trapped," Kit said. "They're going to be coming in through the windows before we know it."

Russ looked around the room and saw a loaf of bread on the counter. He snatched it up and returned to the back door, where the woman was trying to unfasten the lock. He held out the bread, and the woman forgot the lock and yanked the bread out of his hands. She tore through the wrapper and began shoving one slice after another into her mouth, grunting and breathing heavily through her nose as she devoured the loaf. A man walked up behind her and the woman spun on him, raking her nails down his cheeks and clutching the loaf tightly to her body in a protective, greedy stance.

The first freak to show at Kit's house had been a grocery clerk from Mableson's Supermarket, and he'd all but leaped through the door at Kit when he'd opened it. The man, Charlie, according to his name badge, had demanded money. He was hysterical in his command for cash. *Every penny. Every damn penny!*

Then others had come. They fought each other in the yard, and one woman had stabbed another without the least bit of provocation. She'd just walked up behind the woman and driven a knife into her shoulder.

It went downhill from there.

The freaks congregated in the street. Many of them were screaming for money or food or simply shouting

164

obscenities at the different houses. Initially, they'd attacked one another, but now their attention was focused on homes, which included Kit's house and the two boys inside.

In some small way, Russ was relieved. Not because so many people seemed to have lost their minds, but because now he felt certain that his father—for all the ugly things he'd said—was afflicted by this same mania. Russ had to believe his father had meant none of the terrible things but had simply been sick like all of these others.

Still, that didn't exactly help Russ's current situation.

Glass shattered from the front of the house. Russ spun toward the sound. A bright orange light burst on in the living room, followed by a wisp of smoke. Then the sofa began to crackle. One of the freaks had lobbed a bomb into the living room, the kind made with a bottle full of alcohol or gas.

Molotov cocktail, Russ thought.

"They're burning us out," Kit said.

"Then we'd better *get* out," Russ told him.

"What about my mom and my sisters?" Kit cried.

"They aren't here," Russ pointed out. "If they're smart, they're staying put at the supermarket."

"Okay. Okay, let's go."

They ran out the back, knocking the voracious woman into the snow. They leaped the fence separating Kit's yard from the one next door. Russ checked the neighbor's house and saw a long smear of blood running diagonally across a pane of glass. A dark shape moved in another room. He didn't pause long enough to get a good look at it. Instead, he tore through one yard after another, Kit only steps behind him, until they came to the Wellington house on the corner.

There, they found two things of interest. The first was Mrs. Wellington. She was lying in a deep imprint in the snow. She'd been making a snow angel, but now she just lay there staring up into the storm. Russ tried to help her, but she kept saying, "I'm fine. Just fine. Got a little tired and decided to rest. It's so nice to rest." Despite their efforts, neither he nor Kit could get the woman to move, so they left her.

The second thing they found was a snowmobile stashed under a plastic cover at the side of the Wellingtons' house.

"Looks like we got a ride," Russ told Kit.

"Yeah, and where are we supposed to go?"

Russ had thought about that—thought about it a lot. The road out of town was blocked, but there was one place that had only a handful of people and would provide sufficient shelter until the nightmare passed or help arrived:

"The Hawthorn Hotel," he said, yanking the cover off the snowmobile.

The resort was over the ridge and accessible only by a snow-covered road or the tram system, which was down for the day. If they could get to the Hawthorn, they'd be warm and safe at least until morning. The only problem was that they had to go through the village to get there. If this mania had spread throughout the town, they might not make it off Main Street.

"Not bad," Kit said. "Now if we only knew what was happening."

Russ had thought about that too. He was pretty certain he knew what had happened to the people of Winter. He'd heard about it in a class once—at least he'd heard a similar story. He imagined everyone had heard the story once in his or her life, but it was presented as a myth.

It was a myth about a girl. A myth about sin. A myth about a box.

22

The snowfall was easing up, and the white blur of blizzard faded. Emma could see individual snowflakes now. If she were inside and warm and in a world not gone crazy, she would have thought it beautiful. Ahead, she could see the lights at the edge of the village. There was movement in the streets, but it was night now and the figures appeared as nothing more than shadows scurrying about between the buildings. Beyond the shadow play a great orange light flickered, dancing frantically. As they walked down the road, around the bend, Emma saw a building burning in the middle of Main Street.

The whole village is sick, she thought, tears filling her eyes. *It's everywhere.*

On the left she saw the Village Promenade, standing higher than the other structures. Inside were a number of stores designed specifically for the tourist trade—camera shops, souvenir shops, a clothing store with overpriced sweaters and jackets. Thick cables, merely black lines in the purple night, rose from the back of the building and traced lines up the ridge. Normally tram cars ran back and forth on those cables, but her mother had told her the system was down. Nothing was going to be normal tonight.

"Shit," Betina whispered. "It's a war zone down there."

"How . . . ?" Justin said incredulously.

"It spread," Emma said, sniffing back her tears. "God, the whole town."

The long walk through the snow had taken its toll. She was exhausted and cold. The box she carried seemed heavier now—much heavier—as if it had morphed inside the book bag, grown thick and turned to solid lead. Her thighs and ankles ached, and her cheeks burned with cold.

They had to get inside, had to rest. They had to get off the streets and hide and pray they survived the night.

"You okay?" Justin asked.

"Not even close," Betina answered. "My clothes are soaked, and I can't feel my toes. Oh, and there's the whole apocalypse scenario playing out down the road. Where are we supposed to go?"

A gunshot cracked in the night. Its echo bounced off the ridge and filled the valley with ominous sound.

Another followed, and a third.

"People are defending their houses," Justin said, turning his head from side to side to take in the entirety of the village. "I don't think anyone is going to help us. We'd never get close enough for them to see we're normal. We'd better find someplace deserted."

"What about the police station?" Emma offered.

"We don't know if the police are sick or not."

"But we know they have guns," Betina added.

They were now close enough to the village for Emma to hear the riot. Windows shattered and people screamed. Dull shouts, wordless and pained, filled the night.

Emma looked over her shoulder at the empty, snow-covered road winding up behind them. Doug and the others would be coming soon.

A brief flash of red memory—Ernest Banks thrashing in the snow as blood-soaked boots and fists pummeled him—startled Emma. Somewhere behind them was a mob that Emma had already seen murder a man. Ahead of them, the city was in chaos. Hundreds of shadows moved down there, swarming the streets with brutal intent.

Fear returned to her with a desperate immediacy.

She felt exposed and helpless. They had to get off the road.

"Let's circle through the woods," she said. "We can skirt the edge of town and find an empty house on one of the side streets."

"Works for me," Justin said.

"Just get me someplace warm," Betina whispered. Her voice was weak. All the humor and sarcasm had been drained from it.

They left the road and entered the wooded area on the hillside above town. The snow was thick and slowed them down. Above, branches creaked and moaned under the weight of heavy, wet snow. Dark shapes shared the woods with them—tree trunks, broken limbs, boulders. Emma would catch such forms in the corner of her eye and her heart would stutter from dread.

It seemed like they were in the woods for over an hour before they started down toward the neighborhood behind the Main Street shops. They didn't speak during this time, and Emma was careful to make as little noise as possible. Diffused light from the fires on Main Street provided only enough brightness for them to navigate the snowy paths. Even so, night shrouded the wooded area, and there was no way to know with whom they might share it.

Wood snapped behind her and Emma froze in place.

"It's just a branch breaking from the snow," Justin whispered with great certainty.

The sound came again. It was followed by a hushed voice and a nervous laugh.

A moment of absolute stillness followed, so quiet Emma considered the possibility that fear had struck her deaf. Then a voice filled the woods.

"We know you're there," Doug announced, his voice flat and emotionless. "We followed your tracks from the plow. And in case you're wondering, you're totally surrounded."

Suddenly the forest was full of noise. Boys and girls shouted and laughed. Beneath the voices a steady rustling of displaced snow began.

"What do we do?" Betina asked quietly.

I don't know, Emma thought. She felt hands wrap around her arm and jumped before realizing it was just her friend seeking comfort.

"Give us the box," Doug called, "and you can walk out of here. Give us any crap, and we'll shred you right now."

"I think we have to give it to them," Justin whispered.

"We can't hide out here. We'll freeze to death."

Emma clutched the flashlight in her hands tightly, breaking a bit of cold from her fingers. She didn't want to give Doug the box. She couldn't. "They'll just use it again."

"On who?" Justin asked. "Who's left to use it on? The whole town is afflicted."

"But we're not," Betina said. "And I'm not going to be. You want to be some psycho automaton? Fine. Hang here. Emma, if you want to give up, then give me the box."

"I'm not giving them anything," Emma said. "Nothing they want, anyway."

An idea occurred to her. It wasn't a great plan, but it was something.

She turned on the flashlight and waved it around. She pulled away from Betina and Justin and searched the area until she found a crook in the branches of a small aspen tree. Carefully she placed the flashlight in the elbow and backed away. Doug would focus on the light and his pack would gather there. It might give her and Justin and Betina a head start, might allow them to escape.

She was about to wave at her friends to get them to follow her when a fast-moving shape appeared at the edge of the light's beam. Clete Morrisey leaped onto a fallen log behind Justin. He crouched as if ready to spring, but the log was slick with snow and ice. He lost his footing and crashed down on the thick tree trunk. A jagged broken limb stabbed through his side and held him facedown against the log.

Clete screamed and kicked his legs, trying to free himself from the sharp twig. The woods erupted with shouts and the sound of dozens of feet pushing through the snow.

Justin grabbed Betina and dragged her toward Emma. Seeing that her friends were okay, Emma turned to the downhill slope and moved as quickly as she could.

The woods around her came alive. Voices called into the night. Movement in her peripheral vision might have been the teens hunting her, or it might have been nothing more than motionless tree trunks. She couldn't tell and wasn't about to stop to figure it out. Down she raced, half running and half sliding. She rolled over a fallen tree and plopped into a bank of snow, but she didn't let it stop her. She hoisted herself out of the wet mound and slogged ahead.

Justin and Betina were right behind her.

A shadow rose up from the snow ahead of her, but

Emma refused to accommodate the obstacle. She lurched forward and slammed into the shape, sending it backward with a throaty grunt. Hands shot out of the form and grabbed her, pulling Emma down.

"You bitch." It was Doug. She had fallen on top of him, and his hands scrabbled over her shoulders until his fingers locked around her neck.

Emma looked down at him but could barely make out the features because snow had fallen across his face. It didn't matter. Doug was trying to strangle her. She clawed at his wrists and arms, but it seemed futile against the viselike fingers.

"The box is mine," Doug said. "And you're dead meat."

Emma tried to inhale, but the passageway to her lungs was constricted. Her chest began to spasm as her body fought for oxygen. The pain at her neck was hardly noticeable as her thoughts began to swim. A shrill ringing came up in her ears. There was another sound beneath that. Also high, but not quite as sharp as the piercing tone.

Then the hands were gone from her neck. She gasped sweet icy air. It cleared her head immediately, and she realized that the second sound she'd heard was Doug screaming.

Hands were on her shoulders again, but they weren't Doug's. Justin was helping her off the fallen boy. Emma panted for breath. It raked over her damaged throat, but this pain she could handle. She rolled into the snow next to Doug and saw Betina driving her knife into the boy's thigh. Her friend pulled the blade out and stabbed him again.

Laney came screaming out of the woods. Her hands reached out before her like the talons of a hawk. Justin didn't hesitate. He planted his feet in the snow and swung at the girl, hitting her in the stomach with the fireplace poker. He'd swung like he was a baseball star, and Laney doubled over before collapsing.

"Can you move?" Justin asked, looking down at Emma.

"I think so," she replied.

"Then now would be a really good time to do it."

23

Justin had stopped thinking about his father's whiskey or hooking up with Emma. His only thoughts were for survival.

He stepped out of the woods and made sure Betina and Emma were following before setting off across the street. He was grateful the snow had eased up some. The going was still slow, but at least he could see, and the mellower wind didn't bite quite so deeply on his cheeks and chin.

Main Street was two blocks to his left.

The symphony of destruction played on. Fires lit the sky.

A car sped across the far intersection and skidded out of control. It careened sideways through the crossroads and punched through a bank of plowed snow to rest on the front yard of a house. A dozen people chased after the vehicle and descended on it, climbing over the hood and the roof. A man and a woman tried to escape the wreck, only to be shoved to the ground. As Doug's gang had done to Banks earlier that day, the mob descended on the couple and began beating and kicking them viciously. Justin turned away when he saw blood spray over the snow.

Hell, he thought. *We walked straight into hell.*

They found a likely house on the next block. It was a small frame job, similar to many in the village. Unlike the mountain homes, which were designed to impress and lavish comfortable space on their occupants, the village homes were more functional. That meant fewer windows to defend. With any luck, they could hide inside with the lights out and not have to worry about defense at all, though Justin figured this was one step from wishful thinking.

He imagined their biggest concern right now was who might be inside. He didn't have any idea what would happen if he came face to face with a gun-toting homeowner.

"Why here?" Betina asked.

"It's dark," Justin replied. "If anyone's home, it's likely they're hiding like we are. I don't know," he finally admitted. "It just seems like a good place."

"Aren't we too close to the woods?" Betina asked. "They'll just follow us."

"It won't be easy," Emma said, pointing to the road at their feet.

Dozens of footprints dimpled the snow, running in both directions. The street seemed quiet now, but it had seen action recently. Otherwise, snow would have already filled in the prints.

"Let's just get inside," Justin said.

Something flashed in his peripheral vision, and he whipped around to look at the house across the street. The lights inside burned, but there was no other movement. He squinted through the screen of snowflakes, gazing at the side yard, but he saw nothing. He wasn't quite ready to believe it was simply his nerves causing him to see things, but he had yet to see any of the afflicted act with subtlety, and since no one charged at them from across the street, he thought they'd be okay.

Justin was surprised to find the front door unlocked. Once all three of them were inside, he locked the door and prepared himself to take on a freaked resident, but no one screamed or took a shot at them.

"Oh, it's warm," Betina said.

"Yeah, this will work," Justin said. He turned to Emma and tried to read her expression through the gloom. They'd been in such a hurry back in the woods he hadn't even thought to ask if she was really hurt. "Are you okay?"

"Fine," she said. "I need a glass of water, though."

She's kind of amazing, Justin thought. Through everything they'd endured, she'd kept her head on—much more so than he had. Not that he'd been hysterical or had lost it totally, but he'd acted like a tool and it bothered him. He couldn't believe he'd been willing to give up the box and put who knew how many people in danger just to save his own skin. He was embarrassed by his actions and wished he could go back and erase them. He didn't want Emma to think of him as a coward.

"I'll get it," Betina said. "They might have some honey too. That'll help."

"Thanks," Emma said as her friend worked her way across the room to the back of the house.

"Are you sure you're all right?"

"As good as any of us," Emma said. She took the book bag off and dropped onto the sofa. "I'm just so tired."

"Me too," Justin admitted.

"We need a plan," Emma continued. "We've spent so much time running and fighting, we haven't done much on the brain side of things."

"Survival is like that," Justin told her.

"No, survival is using your head," Emma countered. "We've gotten lucky more than once, but that's going to run out. If all of those kids had swarmed us back in the woods—I mean really swarmed us all at once—we'd be dead. Fortunately, insanity makes them less than organized, but we can't keep counting on that."

Again, she was right, and again Justin felt foolish and self-conscious.

"No honey," Betina said, returning to the room with three mugs. "I ran the faucet until the water was reasonably hot. I suppose I could have nuked it, but I'm a little worried about making too much noise, and every button you push makes those things beep."

"Thanks," Emma said, taking the mug from Betina.

Justin took one himself. The warmth felt good in his hands and on his tongue.

Clutching the remaining mug, Betina crossed the room and nodded at the window. "Mind if I close the shades? Someone could see us in here."

"Good idea," Emma agreed.

With the shades closed, the three gathered at the sofa. Justin sat on the cocktail table facing the two girls, trying to think of something intelligent to say, but everything sounded lame in his head.

"Is anyone else thinking about Pandora's box?" Emma asked.

"What?" Justin replied. The question took him completely off guard. Who the hell was Pandora?

"It crossed my mind," Betina said. She sipped from her mug and looked over its edge at Justin.

"I don't follow," Justin admitted.

"Pandora's box," Emma said. "It's a Greek myth. According to the myth, Pandora opened a box and released all of these evil things—greed, gluttony, lust, wrath, and a bunch of others—basically the seven deadly sins. The box was a kind of test for her."

"And she failed," Betina added.

"Right."

"A myth?" Justin asked incredulously. *Is she out of her mind?* "Shouldn't we be focusing on something a little more *real*?"

"Look around," Betina said. "We left real a long way back."

"Myths often have some basis in reality," Emma added. "They get distorted and sometimes amplified, but usually there's a bit of truth in them. What if something like that box Tess opened was the basis for the myth?"

"I don't see it," Justin said cautiously. "All we know

is that a bunch of people are freaking out and Doug is leading a pack of psycho teens trying to get the damn box from us. What does that have to do with deadly sins?"

"The guy in the snowplow," Emma said. "He wasn't freaking out, okay? He was about to have a nap."

"And sloth is one of the deadly sins," Betina said. "Plus, we've got Tess Ward all over Mr. Reed. I'm not sure, but that might count as lust."

"Okay," Justin said, still not sure he was following everything. He didn't know anything about Pandora or the seven deadly sins, and he didn't want to have to confirm his idiocy in their eyes by saying so again. "How did they stop it?"

Emma looked at the book bag and shook her head. "I don't know. I can't even remember where I first heard the myth."

"They didn't stop it," Betina said. "I mean, it was meant to explain why people are such asses to one another, right?"

"It seems more like a curiosity-killed-the-cat kind of story," Emma said. "But the point is, I don't remember anything else about it. It's not something I studied or anything. I just heard about it. But if we can get online, we can get the whole myth. If something like this box was the source for the myth, then it might tell us how to reverse what's happening."

"Then let's see where they keep the computer in this place."

"Or books," Betina said.

"Right," Justin said, "because everyone has books about Greek mythology lying around."

"No," Betina said, "but some people own encyclopedias, especially people over thirty who remember what it was like before the internet. And since this place doesn't exactly scream young and funky MTV junkie, it's possible they actually own books."

"Don't have a fit," Justin said.

"Accept my stressed-out self, and I won't have to hurt you."

Justin rolled his eyes and set off down the hall.

They found a woman in the bedroom at the end of the hall, lying in a bed with the covers pulled up to her wrinkled chin. A cloud of gray hair spilled over her pillow. Justin's first thought was that the woman was dead. Then she opened her eyes and looked at the strangers who had invaded her room. She said nothing, didn't even act surprised.

"We're sorry," Emma said. "We didn't know anyone was home."

The woman closed her eyes and rolled over on her side, away from them, pulling the covers up over her head. Either she sensed no threat or she was just too fatigued to care.

Betina crept across the room to a low bookcase and quickly looked at the titles. Occasionally she threw a glance at the dozing woman as if she expected her to spring from the bed in attack. She must not have found anything useful, because she shook her head and hurried from the room.

Justin backed into the hall. He closed the door and they continued to search the house.

They found an old PC in a nook off the kitchen, and as it booted up, Betina refilled the mugs with hot water. Emma sat before the computer. Her concerned face looked beautiful in the startup glow of the monitor, and Justin felt an overwhelming urge to hold her, to kiss her. But he tamed the feeling and stepped back, crossing his arms over his chest. He looked at the screen, wondering how long the thing would take to come on.

By the time the desktop loaded and the desktop icons popped up, Betina was back with the mugs. Emma clicked on the internet browser icon. Nothing happened.

"She has dial-up," Emma muttered.

A gray box appeared on the screen with the prompt *Dial Tone Not Found*.

"Check the phone," Emma said.

Justin looked around the nook.

"There's one in the kitchen," Betina told him. "On the wall by the microwave."

He left the nook and found the phone. Placing the headset to his ear, Justin heard nothing.

"Crap," he said. "It's out."

"Does your cell phone have internet service?" Emma asked.

"Sure." *Don't they all?*

But when he read the display on his phone, a prompt told him it was searching for service. He punched different buttons futilely. He tried everything, even turning it off and letting it start up again.

"Damn it."

"The relay tower must be out," Betina said. "It's up on the ridge. This happened last year, and the whole place was a dead zone for almost a week."

"Then we have to find someone who's wired through DSL or cable."

"DSL won't work if the phones are out," Betina countered. "It needs to be a cable modem."

"We can't go back out there," Justin said. He knew how weak it sounded, but he didn't care. The violence playing out on Main Street remained with him. He could still see the couple being dragged from their car and beaten into the snow. And that was just on the edge of the village. The shops along Main Street were overrun. People were rioting. The crazies were burning down buildings. For the time being they were safe, and if trouble didn't come looking for them, Justin saw no reason to go looking for it.

"We have to," Emma said. "We could be the only ones who know what's going on. Besides, we have the box."

"I agree with Justin," Betina said. "At least for now. We need to warm up and eat something and put a plan together. We can't keep running around randomly, hoping we can fight our way out every time. We're just going to get weaker."

"But people are killing each other out there."

"And for the reasons you've already said—we know what's going on and we have the box—we don't want to be among the dead."

Emma looked disappointed and a little frantic. Justin hated seeing it. He understood she wanted to help, but getting themselves killed or maimed wasn't going to help anyone. He didn't know if he believed that stuff about Pandora and the box. It seemed pretty out there. Still, the facts and the myth lined up in a couple of places.

"Here's what we know," he said. "We can't communicate with the outside world. Not yet, anyhow. We're exhausted. We're cold. I'm not exactly hungry, but that's probably because I've been so wired for the last few hours. Whatever. We should eat something to keep up our strength. We can take turns trying to get some sleep. Just an hour or two. Once we're in better shape, we can start searching the local houses for an internet setup that works."

Betina nodded her head in agreement, but Emma looked crestfallen—resolved to accept the plan but not liking it at all.

"It's not even seven o'clock," Betina said with a sigh. "It feels like we've been running for days."

Justin checked his watch and saw that she was right. It was ten minutes to seven. The night was just getting started.

They had a plan, though, and Justin thought it was

a good one. He felt pleased with himself for having come up with it.

The feeling passed quickly when he heard a board creak from the front porch.

24

Emma turned quickly to the sound at the front of the house. Though the moaning of wood might have been a trick of the wind, she'd been through too much to ignore it. Justin and Betina had heard it too. Neither of them moved.

The board complained again. Even from their place in the kitchen, they could hear the old doorknob rattle as someone turned it, trying to open the door.

"Shh," Betina hissed. She stood straight-backed and tense, her eyes as big around as golf balls.

As quickly as she could, Emma found the power button for the computer's monitor and punched it, sending the nook into darkness. She turned in the chair and winced at the light squeak the seat made when it revolved. Her pulse beat against her eardrums like the sound of a hovering helicopter. *Whup-whup. Whup-whup.*

The rattling of the doorknob ceased, but Emma continued to hold her breath, listening through the copter-blade rhythm for further signs of intruders. Soon enough, she heard a whooshing in the backyard, snow being pushed ahead of eager bodies. She allowed herself a quick shallow breath.

Justin stood tensed beside her, with the fireplace iron cocked over his shoulder. Betina slid back into the corner, her eyes moving quickly from the window beside Emma to the back door at the edge of the kitchen.

They all heard boots climbing onto the back porch and the click the door made when the knob was turned. To Emma's surprise and dread, it opened.

We didn't check the back door, she thought. The blood beating in her ears sped up—*whupwhupwhup-whup. We're so stupid. So stupid!*

The door swung open.

Justin took a step forward, ready to bring the poker down on someone's head.

"Hello?" a quiet voice—a boy's voice—asked from the threshold. "Hey, we're not freaks or anything. Hello?"

A shadow stepped through the open door.

"Emma?" the quiet voice asked.

Me? she thought. Then something in the voice became familiar.

She heard a scuffling of feet and saw Justin rushing toward the back door, preparing to take on the shadow.

"Wait!" she called.

The kitchen light flashed on just as Justin brought the fireplace iron down, striking Russ Foster's shoulder with a vicious blow. Justin cocked the weapon back, ready to strike again.

"Shit," Russ yelled, holding up his arm to fend off a second attack.

"Stop it," Emma said, leaping from the chair. "Justin, stop. It's Russ."

"So?" Justin asked.

"So," Russ replied, reaching out and yanking the poker from Justin's hand, "I'm not one of those freaks, and I'm not a piñata, so chill out."

Emma joined them at the door. Justin and Russ glared at each other like wrestlers before a cage match. She noticed Russ's friend Kit standing in the middle of the back porch, bent at the knees like he was ready for a race and simply awaiting the firing of a pistol.

"Let them in," Emma said. "Kit, come on. We're okay too."

"They could be lying," Justin noted.

"So could you." Russ pushed his chest out even further. He rubbed his injured shoulder but still looked angry enough for a fight. The poker hung from the hand at the end of his wounded arm. His knuckles were white. "We were trying to get to the tram cars, but the Promenade was overrun with freaks. We bailed across Main and have been hiding out in backyards for over an hour. Then we saw you guys from across the street, and you didn't look all wired like everyone else. We figured it might be a good idea to hook up."

"Get inside," Emma insisted. "We need to get this door locked and this light off. We can talk then." She saw that Justin remained where he was, defiantly. She said his name and touched his shoulder. Her voice or her touch seemed to work. He eased up and backed into the kitchen.

Kit hurried across the porch and joined Russ just inside the door.

Emma closed the door. She turned the lock on the knob and threw the deadbolt, still chastising herself for not having checked the locks before.

We could have been killed, she thought. Then she realized it was still a possibility.

The five of them gathered in the middle of the living

room and sat down. Emma noticed both Russ and Justin were fidgeting, obviously uncomfortable, but Kit was *really* on edge. He tapped the arm of the sofa and kept trying to cross his legs, but he couldn't seem to get comfortable.

"They burned down my house," Kit blurted out. "Torched it. We're like talking in the kitchen and the next thing you know, they gas-bombed the place. It's probably gone now. Totally gone. All of our stuff. Everything. Burned. Ashes. I can't believe it. I don't even know where my family is. They're probably dead. God, they're totally dead."

"Hey, Kit," Russ said, shaking his head. "Be cool. We've all had an exceptionally screwed-up day, and the night's not looking much better. Just keep it together."

"Yeah," Kit agreed. "I need to stay frosty, need to chill. You'd think it would be easy since I've been freezing my ass off for most of the afternoon." He chuckled dryly.

There wasn't a hint of humor in the sound.

"What about you guys?" Russ asked. "How'd you end up here?"

Emma told them what happened, starting with how they'd fled the school. She told them about

Banks, the professor who had looked like Santa Claus and his subsequent death at the hands of Doug and the others.

"No way," Kit said, uttering another of his mirthless cackles. "Dead? Like Doug and Clete and Laney just killed him?"

"Hardly 'just' killed him. They tore him apart," said Justin.

"We've seen some of that," Russ said.

Emma noticed sadness in the boy's eyes. His tense face softened for a moment. He looked like he was remembering someone he loved, then the expression passed.

Who is he thinking about? she wondered.

"Are the phones still out?" Russ asked.

"Yeah," Justin said. "And we can't get on the Web either."

"The Web?" Kit asked.

"We were trying to get some information," Emma said. "But this place only has dial-up."

"What were you looking for?" Russ asked.

Emma was about to tell him, but she suddenly felt embarrassed, as if all of her talk about Greek myths was completely stupid. She didn't know why her throat locked up or why her conviction failed her.

Russ looked so serious, so mature, it just seemed ridiculous to mention an old myth.

But Justin obviously didn't think so. "Pandora's box," he said.

Russ's eyes lit up and he leaned forward. "I was thinking that same thing," he said. "I mean, Tess opening that thing at your place and then all of this happening."

Emma felt a rush of hope burn through her chest. "Do you remember the myth? Do you remember how they stopped it?"

"No," Russ admitted. "I just remember the story. She opens the box and all of these nasty things come out."

"Well, that ranks zero on the help scale," Justin said.

"Yeah, and what's your contribution to the brain bank?"

Justin fell silent and glared at Russ.

"You could cut the testosterone with a knife," Betina muttered. She stood from the sofa and headed toward the kitchen. "I'm going to see what our dining options are. Alert me when the wrestling starts."

"I like her," Kit said, watching Betina's exit. "She's got sass."

"Dude," Russ said. "You need to not talk for a while."

Emma felt the tension in the room growing, and she wanted to defuse it. Things were bad enough outside without bringing the violence indoors. "Why were you going to the tram cars?" she asked.

"We thought we could ride this out at the resort. It isn't open yet, so there aren't many people up there, and it's almost impossible to get to in this weather."

"Apparently, it *is* impossible," Kit added.

"Only because the Promenade was swarming. I think once they empty the place out, they'll move on. We could still make it."

"But the tram isn't running," Emma said. "My mother works at the Hawthorn, and she told me the system was down because of the blizzard."

"Right. I know," Russ said. "But my dad runs the tram. He has for like twenty years. I've watched him do it. It's pretty easy. Just turn it on and hit a couple of buttons."

Emma looked at Justin. "I'll bet they still have internet service and phone service up there. It's on the other side of the ridge."

"They probably have one of those dedicated lines for the internet," Kit said. "I think all companies do now. That way they don't have to share bandwidth or anything."

"You're probably right," she said.

"Wait a minute," Justin interjected. "You're not seriously thinking we should try to get over the ridge?"

"No," Emma replied quickly. "I don't think so. I mean, not yet."

"Good, because it's crazy."

"It's not crazy. Like Russ said, there aren't a lot of people up there, and they may not be afflicted, and more than likely they have a way to communicate with the outside world."

"Exactly," Russ added.

"There are a hundred houses down here that probably have cable internet access."

"Probably," Emma agreed. "But how many of those are being guarded by people with guns? How long before the afflicted people start tearing through them? I don't think going to the hotel is a bad idea, and it's certainly not crazy. It's something to think about if the time comes, that's all."

Actually, Emma thought going to the hotel was a really good idea. She was less thrilled about taking the tram to get there. Ever since childhood she'd been afraid of heights. But that wasn't exactly right. Heights *alone* didn't freak her out. She could stand on a balcony high up and have no problem looking down, but when she was in a small space, suspended over the ground, vertigo kicked in fast and terrifying. It made her freeze in absolute paralysis. It had happened to her when she was a little girl, flying with her mom and dad to see her grandparents, sitting on that plane clutching a stuffed tiger to her chest, feeling certain the plane would fall. It sometimes happened in elevators—especially if the car had glass walls and she could see the ground pulling away from her. Even thinking about it made the room spin a little, so she shook the thought out of her head.

"How did I become a waitress?" Betina asked, walking out of the kitchen. She carried two plates: one piled with lunch meats and cheese, and the other covered in Oreo cookies. A bag of bread hung from her hand. "If you want something to drink there are cans of soda in the fridge."

"Should we ask or something before we take all this woman's food?" Emma asked.

"What woman?" Kit asked. He looked around the room frantically. "Is someone else here?"

"She's vegging," Justin told him.

"Slothing is more like it," Betina corrected. "And I

didn't take *all* of her food. She obviously stocked up recently, probably for the storm. I just grabbed something we could eat that would be quick and wouldn't leave a mess."

Emma felt it was odd to be in a stranger's home, eating someone else's food, while the owner slept in the next room. This was the second house they'd broken into today, and Emma knew it wouldn't be the last.

They hadn't even hesitated to break the law. Sure, it could be put down to survival, and considering all they'd witnessed, their infractions were minor at best. Still, it felt funny—not that they'd broken into the houses, but that they'd done so without asking themselves a single question about it.

In less than a day, the social order in Winter, Colorado, had completely collapsed. Emma couldn't help but wonder how long it would be before the rest of the world followed.

25

Russ couldn't sleep. He was surprised to see Kit snoring lightly, lying on his side next to him. Betina lay in a tight ball across the room. Justin, the rich boy, was standing by the window with his fireplace poker, trying to look tough.

Emma sat curled in a chair with her eyes closed. She was beautiful, serene, but she wasn't asleep, not really. She opened her eyes every couple of minutes. Russ knew because he'd been watching her. How the others could sleep was beyond him. Of course they were exhausted. So was he. But how did you nap through a tornado or a hurricane? How could you shut down like that when everything around you was in turmoil? Considering how tired he felt, he wished he could tune out like Kit and Betina, but there was just no way.

He lay on the floor and threw another furtive glance at Emma, then returned his eyes to the ceiling. He thought about his father, swinging on him with a snow shovel, his face lined with hate and his mouth spewing ugly words. Russ didn't want to believe what his old man had said. More than anything, he wanted his father's rage to be nothing but a side effect of the disease he'd witnessed in so many. But there was probably truth there.

Sorry is marrying some stupid whore. . . .

Sorry is taking care of a worthless punk who ruined your life by being born. . . .

The details were true enough, but was his father's regret? He knew their family had it tough, but Russ had always believed they'd faced it together. He'd never felt like dead weight before, never felt like a burden. But maybe that was how his dad saw it— really saw it.

Russ closed his eyes and bit the inside of his cheek to keep the sadness from bringing a humiliation of tears. He wouldn't cry in front of Emma, and he certainly wasn't going to throw a weep-fest in front of Justin Moore. No way. If rich boy could cope, so could Russ.

He was worried about Kit, though. His friend had always been hyper, getting excited about the smallest stuff, but it was different now, like the stress had eroded his logic until it was brittle and ready to snap. He needed to keep an eye on him; that was all. Kit had seen his house set on fire, seen his home reducing to smoke and ash and garbage. He didn't even know where his parents were, let alone if they were okay. They could have been two more crazies in the streets, or two more victims. At least Russ knew where his father was. He just hoped the old man was okay and would manage to stay okay until someone figured out how to stop all of this.

Russ rolled over and got his feet under him. He stood. Walking toward the window, he noticed Justin stiffen up as if Russ were some kind of threat. *Good,* Russ thought.

"We should probably wake everybody up," he whispered.

"Let them rest. They're exhausted."

"Yeah, but if we're going to head out, we should do it before the storm picks up again."

"The storm is slowing down," Justin argued.

"No, it's not. This is like the eye of a hurricane. The worst is just getting started."

"You don't know that."

"Yeah, well, I've lived here my whole life, and I know these storms. The blizzard is going to kick into high gear again tonight, and it's going to go until morning. So if we're planning on trekking around the neighborhood to find a computer that works, we should get going."

"What? You think you're calling the shots now?"

"Don't even," Russ said, trying to keep his voice under control. He didn't want people to wake up to a fight. "You guys made the plan. I'm just sticking to it."

"But you just came across town. We had to fight our way down the mountain, being hunted by Doug and his mentally deficient posse. We about froze to death and nearly got ourselves torn apart, so I think Emma and Betina deserve a break."

"Keep it down," Russ said. He looked around the room and realized it was too late for that. Kit and Betina were awake, staring at them. Emma sat in her chair, eyes open but trying not to look at them.

"Way to go," Justin said, stepping away from the window.

"Me?" Russ said. He shook his head and let the argument drop. Justin seemed to be about as nuts as the people outside.

"What time is it?" Emma asked.

"A little after nine," Justin told her.

Emma stood up and stretched. Russ watched the graceful display from the corner of his eye, noticing the way her breasts pushed at her sweater and the way her neck curved as she bent her head to the side, working the blood back into her muscles.

"We should get going," she said. "Is it still snowing?"

Russ opened the curtain and peered outside. Snow dappled the air, drifting like soft confetti toward the blanket of white covering the yards and the roads.

"It's not bad yet. But it's supposed to get worse."

"Then we really need to head out," Emma said.

"I need coffee," Betina said, climbing to her feet.

"Starbucks is closed," Kit replied. "Everything is closed. It's all just cinder and ash."

Russ looked at his friend. Kit's eyes were blank. As he got to his feet, he moved like an old man whose joints were giving him pains.

"You okay?" Russ asked.

Kit fixed cold, vacant eyes on Russ.

"Nothing's okay," Kit said. "What a stupid thing to ask."

26

Outside again. Emma was cold, but it wasn't the bone-biting freeze she'd felt before they'd found shelter in the slothing woman's house. Though she hadn't slept, she felt rested and her head was clearer. The book bag on her back felt lighter than it had; the box had lost its leaden heaviness. Despite the chill, she was glad to be out of the house. Justin and Russ seemed about ready to fight. Emma didn't know what the boys' problem was, but the tension coming off them was palpable and unnerving. And something was wrong with Kit, Emma knew. He wasn't acting deranged like the crazies were, but he wasn't coping.

As they walked, they stayed close to the houses. The snow was deeper in the yards than on the streets, but they didn't want to be caught out in the open. They crept through the shadows, seeking empty homes, hoping one would have a link to the outside world. They'd already traveled two blocks with no luck. Either someone was obviously hiding in the house, or—as happened on one occasion—they'd opened a front door only to find themselves staring down the barrel of a shotgun. The owner of the house didn't say a word, just aimed his gun at them. Nothing really needed to be said. They backed out of the house, closing the door behind them, and hurried away.

Of the four houses they'd actually gone into, only one had a working computer. The others had been smashed or stolen, leaving behind torn cables and empty desks. Emma had tried to log on to the Web but couldn't get the modem to respond: no signal. Betina hadn't had any better luck finding books that might help them.

Farther down, they saw the fires burning on Main Street over the roofs of the ranch houses on Mesa Drive. At the intersection of Mesa and Arapahoe, Emma looked to her left. Except for the fires, Main Street seemed quiet. The manic horde seemed to have moved on or settled down.

Maybe it's over, Emma thought. *Maybe it was all just temporary, a fleeting moment of insanity, a single mad day.*

Or maybe they all killed one another.

Suddenly, a gunshot exploded two blocks behind them, telling Emma the siege continued. She wondered if it had come from the house they'd tried to enter. Another shot followed, and she supposed it didn't matter.

The gunshots acted like a mating call, though. Violence summoning violence. Suddenly the distant intersection where Arapahoe met Main Street was teeming with frantic people. Lights from the fires danced over the buildings at their back, casting the mob in shadow. They raced forward. Emma thought there had to be a hundred of them, pouring onto the side street like a dark flood.

"Go back," Justin said, waving his hands to Emma and the others. "Go back. Go back."

Emma turned on her heels. Russ's arm locked around her, and he all but dragged her away from the curb, cutting close along the porch of the house on the corner. They ran behind Betina and followed as Kit dashed into an alley between two of the low houses.

Another gunshot echoed in the night and brought a furious roar from the crowd.

Emma half ran and half jumped through the snow that had drifted between the houses. The book bag bounced against her back and she grabbed one of the straps, fearing it might fall off if she didn't secure it.

The five of them emerged into a backyard, and she was relieved to see the high fence on the side, separating the yard from the marauding lunatics on the road. Ahead, Betina and Kit broke to the left and fell beneath the cover of shadows. Russ helped her over a low fence into the neighboring yard. Justin hopped the fence and tore after Betina and Kit. He reached a high fence just as Kit flipped over the top of it. Then Justin leaped, grabbed the edge, and pulled himself over. It wasn't as easy for Betina. She struggled to climb the obstruction, but her feet kept slipping. Emma got below Betina's scrabbling feet and gave her a shove. Her friend sailed up and over the fence.

Then Emma leaped for the fence. Her fingers scraped over the top and she fell back. Ice and snow slicked the wood. Russ grabbed her, lifting beneath her arms. She turned her head to him and saw the silhouettes of the marauding mob filling the alley between the two houses, following the path they'd cut through the yards.

Her heart leaped into her throat, but she didn't stop to process her fear. If she had, it would have killed her.

Instead, she turned back to the fence and let Russ support her feet as she climbed over. She dropped

209

into more snow and looked back, waiting for Russ to climb over. The sounds from the running people grew. Groans and screams and meaningless chants came to her on the cold air.

Russ flew over the fence and landed next to her. Heavy bodies hit the barrier a moment later, sending it rocking on its posts toward them. Wood splintered and complained, but the fence held.

"Run," Russ said.

Justin, Kit, and Betina waited at the corner of the house for them. When they caught up, all five eased along the alley. Emma cast rapid glances over her shoulder to make sure the fence behind them was holding. Ahead was Portsmouth Street, which ran between Main and Mesa.

A man walked into their path twenty feet ahead.

A flashlight beam cut into Emma's eyes, and she shielded them with her palm.

"Freeze," the man said. "Winter Police. Stay right where you are."

His name was Dan Margolin. He was a rookie with the Winter Police Department and the only officer left—that he knew of—who hadn't completely lost his mind. He was boyish and handsome, Emma thought, and he'd been as unnerved by Emma and her friends as they were by him.

"I've given up trying to patrol," Margolin said, leading them onto Portsmouth Street. "Forget about crowd control. Whatever's happening here has happened fast. We tried to get the word out, you know, telling people to get inside and lock the doors, but I don't know if it did any good."

"Where are we going?" Russ asked.

"The Promenade," Officer Margolin said.

"Whoa," Russ said. "Kit and I were there and it was a total war zone."

"Not anymore. Main Street has been stripped clean. My vehicle is stashed in the Promenade garage. If it's still running, I'm getting you folks up the hill and away from this mess."

"Is the pass still closed?" Emma asked.

"Yeah. It's down for the count. We had another avalanche just before things fell apart."

"So are they working on it?" Justin asked.

"Working on it?" Margolin replied. "Who? Who the hell is left to work on anything? The crew got out of there just before a new wall of snow came down. By the time the powder settled, half of them were trying to kill the others."

"Just asking."

"Look, I'm not trying to be an ass, okay?" Margolin said. "Everything is broken right now. I'm surprised we still have power, but that'll probably go, once the second wave of snow hits. That will mean we're in the dark with those things out there, and I don't much like the idea of that."

"Did anyone get a message out?" Russ wanted to know. "You know, a radio message or email or something to let someone know what's going on here?"

"I managed to get a call to the state police before our captain started shooting everything that moved."

"That's good."

"It's something," Margolin said. "But the fact is, they don't have any way to reach us. The passes are a mess, the road is blocked, and they aren't going to be sending helicopters through a blizzard. Even if they did, they couldn't get enough men on those birds to handle this."

"We were thinking about the resort," Russ said, his steps crunching in the snow.

Margolin paused for a moment and looked up at the ridge. At night, the blanket of snow looked pale plum, rising in vast sheets to a ghostly mist near the crest.

"Not a bad idea," he said. "But the route hasn't been plowed in about ten hours. I doubt even four-wheel drive could get through it, and it certainly wouldn't be running fast enough to outpace those lunatics. We'd probably end up trapped inside. The last report we got from the plow crews indicated that Wolff Road was clear, almost to the peak. We stand a good chance of making high ground before the blizzard cranks up again."

We spent all of that time coming down the mountain, Emma thought, *and now we're just going back up?* She didn't like the idea. If the road was clear enough for them to get through, then it was clear enough for the afflicted to follow. And when they got up there, then what? Hide in another house until they were discovered? She knew Officer Margolin meant well, and his plan might work, but she wasn't comfortable with the suggestion.

"Is everyone sick?" Russ asked. "I mean, except us."

"No," Officer Margolin said. "We've got at least seven thousand year-round residents in the valley. If everyone was affected, I imagine this place would have been reduced to rubble hours ago. We were still getting calls right up until the phones went out. Hundreds of them. Mostly, people are locked in their homes, defending themselves." The police officer crossed a yard and pressed himself to the side of a house, peering around the corner and holding his hand up for Emma and the others to wait.

The five huddled close, looking expectantly at the young officer. Emma held Betina's shoulders and pressed close to the siding.

"Okay," Officer Margolin said, stepping around the side of the house.

Main Street was one block down. The Village Promenade stood ahead of them to the left on the far corner of the intersection. The mall itself had been cute. It wasn't anymore. Lights still blazed inside, but that was perhaps the only thing normal about the scene. The shops' windows had all been shattered. Display racks lay on their sides amid shards of glass and jagged debris. Snow blew through the openings, drifting against the battered counter of the Snap! Photo Shop and naked mannequins lying like corpses in the women's clothing store. It looked like bombs had gone off in each of the stores, destroying the contents but leaving the walls standing.

Officer Margolin edged them onward, his gun close to his side, his head moving slowly, taking in his surroundings with measured glances.

"The parking garage is around back," Justin whispered behind Emma, pointing to the roof of a concrete structure on the far side of the Promenade.

Emma nodded. "I know. We just have to get there."

Betina was the first to see the man stumbling across the street ahead of them. He carried a cash register in his arms like a fat, angular baby. Betina stopped and said, "Oh, hell." Emma ran into her back and came to a halt.

Officer Margolin eyed the man and lifted his weapon. "Stay where you are," he ordered, aiming along the barrel at the shambling man.

That's Tess Ward's father, Emma thought. She recognized him from the parent-student orientation at the beginning of the school year.

Now he was walking through ankle-deep snow, struggling with the cash register's weight. Money—dollar bills, tens, and twenties—poked from his pockets and the lapels of his ski parka. He was almost halfway across the street when he finally noticed Officer Margolin and the rest of them.

Mr. Ward dropped the cash register. It crunched into the snow. He raised a small black gun and pointed it at Officer Margolin.

"Drop your weapon," Margolin said.

"Cash," Mr. Ward said, waving his gun through the air, brushing aside falling snowflakes as he displayed his weapon. "Empty your pockets. I want cash, cell phones, and jewelry. Do it now!"

"Sir, I'm going to ask you again to drop your weapon. Then I will be forced to take action."

Mr. Ward continued his clumsy approach, waving his gun in a flat figure-eight pattern, like he was trying to aim at a circling fly. "Empty your pockets."

"Drop your weapon!"

A gun's report cracked, riding crisp on the thin, frigid air.

Mr. Ward wobbled for a moment. He pulled the trigger of his gun. *Click. Click. Click.* Then he fell facedown on the road. Several bills knocked loose and littered the snow around him. Blood from the hole in his chest melted the snowpack like acid.

"Damn," said Kit uneasily.

Emma felt far too little about the incident. After all that had happened, one more note of violence barely registered. In fact, recognizing how calmly she had accepted the aggression bothered her more than the violence itself.

"Man, I wish you hadn't had to see that," Officer Margolin said.

He crouched low and slid along the side of the building and craned his neck to look around the corner down Main Street. His shoulders stiffened, and he pulled away from the edge.

He looked at Emma, then at the others.

"I think we're in trouble," he said.

27

Justin stared at the dark lump in the snow. Only a moment before it had been walking around, a man carrying a cash register and a gun, a man hoarding cash anywhere he could stash it. Justin didn't know who the guy was before all of this happened, but at one point, he'd been a man, and now he was a heap in the snow. Justin couldn't take his eyes away from the guy, even when that cop said something about trouble.

Justin felt the urge to walk up to the fallen man. Maybe he wasn't dead, maybe just injured. Part of his mind understood it was ridiculous. The guy would have shot him for the money in his wallet.

Too many people are dead, he thought. *Too many more are going to die.*

"Justin," Emma said.

Her voice came from behind him. He loved her voice. He didn't want to see her end up another lump in the snow, and he didn't want to become one himself.

Movement all around snapped him from the fugue of shock. He was momentarily disoriented and suddenly felt colder than he had all day.

"Justin," Emma repeated.

He looked around, still confused. They were standing next to the Winter United Bank building. Catty-corner from them, the Village Promenade rose as the last retail space on Main Street. Across Main Street was the hollowed-out shell of a men's clothing store.

Justin checked their backs. Only a block away, he saw people moving. The mob that had chased them through the yards emerged from a side street. He turned to the cop, about to suggest they run their asses off—then he saw the people moving in from Main Street.

We're trapped, he thought. *It's over.*

Two packs of crazies were converging on the corner where Justin and the others stood. The faces he saw were painted in dancing flames from the burning buildings. They all looked sick, drained. Their eyes were wild, moving rapidly back and forth as if watching rats scurry over the snow. They moved in a slow, confident wave to the intersection. They were all talking. The sounds weren't the desperate cries he'd heard earlier but rather controlled mutterings, like each member of the crowd performed a different chant, creating a totally freaky, droning chorus.

Officer Margolin stepped away from the side of the building. Russ and Kit followed the cop into the street, moving quickly to keep as much distance as possible between themselves and the two groups of lunatics. Justin did the same, quickly checking over his shoulder to make sure Emma was also following.

"No way I'm going to be able to manage this," the cop said, just loud enough for Justin to hear. Russ stepped up close to the officer, and they exchanged a brief whispered conversation.

The cop shook his head.

The crowd of crazies just watched. Manic eyes burned from emaciated faces, observing the six normal people backing through the intersection. The afflicted looked dead. They all looked dead and sick and insane. There had to be fifteen of them on Main Street and another dozen moving in from Portsmouth.

"What are we doing?" Justin said through a tight, trembling jaw.

"Looking for a hole," Officer Margolin replied. "I'm not ready to give up yet."

From the middle of the intersection, Justin had a

clear view of Main Street. Behind the growing wall of people, it looked like a war zone. The road was littered with debris and glass and bodies. Flames still jumped from the Parka Lot and Skis 'n' Things next door. Across the street, to Justin's left, another fire was beginning to eat its way up the side of Elmer's Fudge Shop. At the end of the block, in the next intersection, a snowplow faced them, idling and puffing exhaust and steam into the night. Its headlights and fog lights blazed through the lace of falling snow. A figure stood in the bath of light.

She was tall and slender, and though Justin could not make out her features well because of the harsh light behind her, he knew it was Tess Ward. She stood with her arms at her side, her head cocked slightly.

The dark figures from the side of the building merged with those in the middle of Main Street. Doug Nichols led them. The boy limped badly from the stab wounds Betina had given him. A shirt or towel was wrapped around his thigh, and he dragged the wounded leg, using it only to support himself as he lurched forward with the uninjured one.

The other kids from school were there as well, except for those who had fallen during the pursuit.

Tess began to walk forward. The snowplow at her

back revved its engine and crawled along behind her like a prehistoric pet.

"This is it," Betina said.

"Shh," Emma warned.

Russ grabbed Kit's shoulder and hauled him away from Officer Margolin in Justin's direction.

"He's going to try to distract them," Russ said.

"He's going to try to distract *all* of them?"

"I know," Russ whispered, "but look, if we can get in the tram building, the door has a good lock on it. We can't keep them out forever, but we might be able to hold them off long enough to get the system running."

"No way," Justin said. It was crazy. They wouldn't even make it to the building, let alone have time to get the machinery running and the trams operational.

"No choice," Russ said. "It's about to go off. Just follow Kit and me. There's an entrance on the side."

"It won't work," Justin argued.

"It's all we've got."

Justin checked the mob on the street in front of them, then threw a glance at the big wooden building beside the Village Promenade. *No way*, he thought. Not unless Officer Margolin was a superhero shot and fired off some rounds to blow up a few of the cars on

Main Street. Plus, they'd have to get lucky enough to have bits of shrapnel knock out at least three quarters of the crowd.

"Get the box," Tess called. Another minute and she'd be at the back of the gathered lunatics.

Doug was already limping forward. Three of his pack peeled away from the crowd and followed. Laney was there. So was Laurent from Justin's science lab and Milda from the yearbook committee.

"Give it to us," Doug said. With the fire behind him he looked like a demon emerging from hell.

"Stay right where you are," Officer Margolin ordered. "Don't force me to shoot."

"Do you have a hundred bullets, Officer?" Doug asked. "Do you have a thousand? A million?"

"I have enough," Officer Margolin said.

He shot Doug in his good leg. Pure surprise flashed over Doug's face as he collapsed to the road. The other crazy people stopped. They looked at Doug like he was an interesting piece of litter, then they continued forward.

"Bring me the box," Tess shouted.

"Wait," Officer Margolin called. "I don't want to see anyone else get hurt. Let's just talk about this."

Tess continued walking forward. Her steps were

smooth and graceful, nothing like the sickly limp she'd had at school that morning. Whatever was wrong with her, she seemed to be adapting to it.

"Just stay where you are," Officer Margolin said. "No one else has to get hurt tonight. Return to your homes."

Justin couldn't believe the cop was trying to reason with this crowd. Though the freaks had stopped moving forward—all except Tess—the eagerness for action showed in their ill faces. They wanted violence. Justin didn't know what was holding them back, but he felt certain it wouldn't last.

Tess reached the back of the mob and it parted for her like a gate. She continued forward, toward Officer Margolin, who aimed his pistol at the approaching girl.

Justin finally got a clear look at Tess, and he wished he hadn't. Not only did she look disgustingly thin, but her face now wore a grotesque silver mask. It moved and shifted as if made from liquid. Trails of motion along her cheek, like fresh cuts, drew his attention, and he realized that Tess wasn't wearing a mask at all. The silver creatures from the box—the swarm—covered her face, slinking and sliding over it. In fact, the things covered every bit of exposed skin, making her shimmer in the dancing firelight. Bits of silver also filled the air around her, circling her head like flies.

She was hosting the terrible swarm—and feeding it.

"Don't take another step," Officer Margolin called. "I'll be forced to shoot."

One of the silver specks, discernible from the snowflakes only by the fact that it flew upward and caught the light, rocketed from the swarm. It arced like a tiny missile, heading directly for Officer Margolin. A moment later, the cop recoiled and threw one hand to his face. He called out obscenities and spun in a tight circle as if stung by a bee.

That's how she's controlling them, Justin thought. *That's why they're going crazy. It's those things from the box. They're living in Tess, and she's been spreading them all over town. That's why I'm okay, even though I was right there. They needed a host first.*

Tess looked directly at Justin then. The corners of her metallic mouth lifted in a sick grimace.

Under the attention of this nightmarish girl, Justin's blood ran cold. He stumbled backward.

She's going to kill me, he thought. *She's going to kill us all.*

Officer Margolin continued to struggle with the silver

speck that had attacked him, and the scene around Justin went crazy. Someone yanked at his collar and he nearly fell backward. He spun around and saw that Russ was tugging him toward the Promenade. Justin tried to run, but a foot slipped out from under him and he nearly crashed to the street. He skidded a moment, righted himself, and tore off toward the far corner. The screeching, moaning sounds of the afflicted rose into the crisp air, surrounding him like a shrill cloud. Beneath these animal cries was the rhythmic stomping of dozens of feet in the snow.

"Run. Run. Run!" yelled Russ.

In his confusion, Justin had been slow to respond. His brain sent panicked signals to his legs—faster, faster—as he charged for the boxy wooden building beside the Promenade.

Russ and Kit disappeared around the corner of the tram station. Justin caught up with Emma and Betina just as the girls took the turn.

Betina screamed. Emma cried out a second later.

In the bath of floodlights at the building's side, a woman squatted in the snow. She was short, maybe thirty years old, with spiky brown hair and wearing nothing but a thin cotton dress. Her mouth was smeared with blood and gore and bits of fur. She chewed hungrily, holding something dark in her hands.

The girls kept screaming, and Justin understood the need. His stomach rolled and he bit down on the nausea, trying to keep from being sick. He turned away from the ravenous woman to find Russ standing in an open doorway, waving at them.

"Go," Justin said, knocking Emma and Betina on the backs.

Their shock broke. Both girls raced for the door, and Justin followed. It sounded like the mob was only a step behind him.

As he entered the tram station, someone else ran out.

It was Kit. He slammed into Justin's shoulder, sending him hard against the doorjamb. The boy kept running, back into the snow and right into the crowd.

"Close the door," Justin said, spinning away from the jamb and into the building.

"Kit!" Russ called.

But it was too late. The pack of lunatics had the boy. They surrounded him, fell on him like a wave, knocking Kit to the snow.

"Close the door!" Justin yelled. He shoved Russ, who stood stunned, out of the way and threw the door closed. Russ was trying to grab him. A fist landed on Justin's ear, making it ring, but he had to secure the door. Somehow they'd made it inside. Another moment of safety.

"Kit is out there," Russ bellowed.

"And so are *they*."

"It was a dog," Betina cried behind them. "She was eating a dog. Who could do that?"

"Damn it, my friend is out there."

"He's dead," Justin said. "Or he's one of them."

"You son of a bitch," Russ shouted in his face. "You don't care about anyone but yourself. You selfish dick-head."

"We're alive, aren't we?"

Russ grabbed him by the jacket and threw Justin back into the wall. The boy's eyes radiated fury. His jaw clenched tightly as if he were trying to keep from screaming. Justin's mind scrambled with panic. He'd escaped a mob of lunatics only to find himself trapped inside the building with another one.

The crying and yelling continued. It came at Justin like fists, hitting first on the left and then the right. Russ was shouting about his lost friend. Betina wailed over the death of a pet and the woman who'd turned the animal into a meal. He couldn't make sense of what was going on and felt his head growing light with the struggle.

"Stop it!" Emma cried. The entryway became quiet, though the sounds of chaos raged beyond the door. "There's nothing we can do about Kit," she continued. "And we don't have a lot of time."

Russ gave Justin a final searing glare before releasing him. He punched the door twice. Hard. Justin moved away from the wall, knowing Russ could turn that aggression on him again.

"Now, how do we get to the tram?" Emma asked.

"It's upstairs," Russ said miserably, leaning on the door for support. "We need to get some boxes in front of this door first or they'll get through it."

"Are there any other doors?" Justin asked.

"Well, there's the main entrance," Russ said sarcastically. "You know, where people come through to ride the tram?"

"You don't have to be an ass."

"Just shut up," Russ said.

Russ stepped away from the door and turned to a panel in the wall. He pulled back a flat metal door the size of a paperback novel. Quickly he punched a series of buttons to deactivate the alarm.

"The other door," Emma said, "it's not glass, is it?

Like the rest of the Promenade?"

"No, it's a big wooden door. It was the original entrance. It's more secure than this one. This was here before the Promenade, and they reinforced that door to keep intruders out. A security guard used to stay down here before they got this alarm system. If they locked the place up properly, this is the door we have to worry about."

"So what do we use to block it?" Emma asked.

Justin couldn't help but note how logical Emma was being. She'd been as freaked out as Betina about seeing that woman outside but, unlike Betina, who still wept and shook her head in disbelief, Emma was already focused on their next moves.

Russ looked around the room. Justin did the same.

He couldn't see well. The only light came from a low-watt bulb in the ceiling, which cast a sickly yellow glow that didn't seem to reach the floor. The room looked like an old storage shed, just thick planks running floor to ceiling to make walls. A steep staircase, also wood and looking rickety, ran up the far wall and stopped at a doorway on the second floor. *This must be where the control room is located.* Stacks of cardboard boxes, some of which were coming apart at the edges, stood against a wall. None of them looked strong enough to hold their contents if moved, let alone add any real security as a blockade.

Fists began pounding on the door beside him, and Justin leaped back.

"We'd better find something," Russ muttered, stalking away from the wall and venturing deeper into the room.

"Justin," Emma said, "can you watch the door?"

He agreed, though he had no idea what he could do if they started breaking through. He pushed his back against the door and wedged his feet as he watched Emma and Betina follow Russ into the gloom.

28

Russ stood in the security office feeling sick. His best friend was gone. First his dad and now Kit. Maybe they were still alive and would remain that way until a cure could be found. If there *was* a cure. If there was any way to stay alive among those raving monsters. Russ had no way to know. The one thing he did know was that he didn't trust Justin. Back in the neighborhood, before they'd run into Officer Margolin, Justin had about knocked Russ over while fleeing the crowd of crazies. The jerk didn't even try to help Betina or Emma over the fence. He'd just hopped it himself and kept running to save his own ass.

Russ noticed an ax propped against the wall, next to an old and rusted snow shovel a lot like the one his father had used when attempting to open his skull. Russ grabbed the ax and held it tightly, testing its weight in his hand.

He couldn't believe Kit was gone. What had happened? They'd been the first two inside the tram building. Russ remembered Kit was babbling about something, but he had been too distracted, trying to get everyone inside, to pay attention. The next thing he knew, Justin was walking in, and Kit was running out.

Why? Had his friend just snapped? Or was it an act of heroism, throwing himself at the mob to give the others a chance to lock themselves in? Russ wanted to believe the latter, but he just didn't know.

He put away his pained thoughts and began looking around the room. There was a desk and a chair, a few spare tools lying around. A refrigerator—once white, now filthy—stood in the corner. It was a squat machine, standing only as high as Russ's chin, but it was deep and appeared to have thick walls. That and the desk would probably do the trick. They'd have to. There was nothing else around.

He put the ax down and waved for Emma and Betina to join him.

Ten minutes later, they were all upstairs. The tram room was designed with catwalks on either side of the car bays. It had a vast opening on the back face of the building through which the cars, suspended on thick cables, entered and exited. The dock stood twenty feet off the ground and had been designed to keep the curious from climbing up the supports. One car was docked in the bay. The other would be on the resort side. As he'd suspected, the door to the Promenade was secure. Even if the mob went through the shopping area, they'd find an impenetrable barrier.

Emma stood at the window and Justin chopped at the topmost stairs with the ax just in case the crazies got through the door below. Russ found the lockbox affixed to the wall and opened it with the small key he kept for his father. Like the door below, Russ had a key to everything in the tram building—security in case his father lost his own set, which happened often enough. The only key he didn't have was the one that unlocked the tram-operating panel, but he knew a spare was kept in the lockbox.

At the window, Emma gasped.

"What's going on?" Russ asked, retrieving the key.

"They're killing Doug," she whispered. "Tess pointed at him, and a bunch of people went over and started beating him like they did with that professor."

"He let her down when he failed to retrieve the box," Betina said. She chewed on a hangnail, cringing by the window. "She always acted like the queen of the city. Now she is."

"How does she control them?" Emma said, turning to her friend. "I mean, they were totally out of control, but she gets them to do what she wants."

"It's those silver things," Justin said. "I saw one attack the cop. They're living in Tess like she's some kind of hive. That's how it spread. Tess walked around all night infecting who she could and then she showed up at school this morning. That's why people who weren't even at the party, like Banks and those freaks outside, got sick when the rest of us didn't."

"So she's a carrier," Betina said. "Like with a virus?"

"Right."

Russ hated to admit it, but Justin was probably right. That morning he'd seen something silver creeping over Laney Hoffman's cheek and he'd written it off as glitter. And Kit had said something similar earlier in the day to explain Vic Hoffman's behavior at the fudge shop, but Russ had dismissed it as more of Kit's conspiracy babble.

Damn, he wanted to hear that crap again. If they somehow got through all of this and Kit was okay, he'd never laugh at the kid's out-there speculations again.

He turned the key and powered up the control panel. He tried to remember the steps his father had shown him so many years ago. Basically, the tram system was all automated. Once it got moving, they wouldn't have to do anything. The car would leave this station, rise over the ridge, and deposit them on the other side. The doors opened automatically at each end. Someone had to operate the buttons to close the doors and, in the case of emergencies, open them again, but once they got inside, Russ couldn't imagine a reason they'd want those doors open again until they were well over the ridge.

"How much longer?" Betina called.

"A couple of minutes. How's it look down there?"

"The lock is giving."

"If they aren't through yet, we'll make it," Russ told her, more to ease everyone's mind than anything else. He actually had no idea how much longer the process would take.

He pushed a button, and the engines cranked on. He waited to see if they'd cut out, feeling certain their luck had finally left them, but the engines continued grinding away.

"The engines need a couple minutes to warm up," Russ said, stepping away from the panel. "This system's old, and we don't want to take any chances with it."

"You'd think they'd have a new one," Justin said.

"They will next year," Russ told him. "Be glad they didn't change it out yet. I wouldn't have a clue how a new system operated. I only know this one because I used to watch my dad."

Russ left the control panel and crossed to the window. He leaned over Emma's shoulder, brushing up against her back as he did so. The contact was welcome, but he didn't allow himself to enjoy it. He repositioned himself so they weren't touching, and looked out into the street.

Tess stood below the window, staring up at them. She wore a long white down coat that had been shredded. Tufts of feathers puffed from the jacket's quilting. Strips of fabric hung in tattered fringe. The collar had been torn or cut in a ragged pattern. The serrated edge rose like a battered crown from her shoulders. Doug's remains lay in the snow at her feet. A blast of wind sent a sheet of snow across the scene, and for a moment Russ thought Tess had disappeared, but he'd witnessed no magic. When the gust passed, Tess remained on the street below.

"They're coming in," Justin shouted. "The door's giving way."

"Okay, time to travel," Russ said. He ran back to the control panel. "Lock that door," he called to Justin as he pressed a yellow button.

The tram car doors opened. "Everyone get inside," he yelled.

Justin ran past Emma and Betina and crossed into the car. The girls remained by the window.

"Come on," Russ insisted.

"She isn't good with heights," Betina called.

Russ looked at Emma. All of the color was out of her face. She stared at the tram car like it was a monster, the open doors its mouth waiting to swallow her whole. It seemed ridiculous that an irrational fear should overpower the real thing, but Russ wasn't a psychologist. He didn't know how these things worked. He just knew they had to move.

He left the booth and walked up to Emma. He grabbed her shoulders and made sure she was looking at him when he said, "There has never, ever been an accident on this system. It's never even locked up before. My dad was really proud of that fact."

"I know," Emma said. "I just can't make my legs move."

Russ nodded. "Can I move you?"

"What?"

"I can carry you."

"That won't help."

"We don't have time for this."

"I know. I know."

Emma swallowed hard and took her first step toward the car. Betina grasped her friend's elbow and guided her forward, urging her to move faster. With each step, Emma looked a shade greener, like she was about to be sick.

Once they reached the tram car, Emma tried to back away. "You guys go. Take the box. I'll do what I can here."

"Don't be stupid," Russ said. "Once they get in, they'll be up here."

"But Justin broke the stairs."

"Only the top few," Russ said. "Only enough to slow them down. It won't keep them out. Come on, Emma. We aren't going to leave you."

A desperate thought passed through Russ's mind. He could punch Emma. Knock her out. Then she wouldn't have to fear the ride over the ridge. *That's what they'd do in a movie,* he thought. But he couldn't hit her, not for any reason.

"Please," he said. "If you don't get in the car, none of us are leaving."

This seemed to work. Emma bit down on her lower lip and nodded her head. She closed her eyes and walked backward into the car.

Relieved, Russ waited for Betina to get inside. The

three stood at the back of the car, watching him as he returned to the booth.

They'd been through a lot together.

He was going to miss them.

Russ hit a white button and the doors closed. He didn't look up to see the others' reaction. Muffled cries came from the car, but he refused to acknowledge them, even with a glance. If he saw Emma again, he might change his mind and then they'd all be doomed. He had to stay behind. Alone.

Someone had to close the doors.

Someone had to make sure the crazies didn't destroy the system or shut it down while the tram was hanging over the ridge.

Besides, he didn't have much to look forward to, even if Emma and the others found a cure. Kit was gone. Russ's father might be okay, but he'd never be able to look at him the same again.

This was better.

This was easier.

He kept his head down until the car was out of the bay. By the time he looked up, it was just a smudge in a flurry of white.

29

Emma looked through the tram window at Russ, who stood with his head down, eyeing the control panel in the booth. Her terror at being in the car was momentarily forgotten as she called for the boy who remained behind.

"Russ, stop the tram. You can't stay here by yourself. Russ!"

Next to her Betina also cried out, beating on the window to get Russ's attention. Her friend sounded angry, but Emma's own voice was fueled with grief. Justin stood next to them quietly, pressed to the glass inset of the door.

A tremendous sadness opened in Emma's chest. She was so tired of the misery and the fear. All she wanted to do was cry, because it felt like the despair was eating a hole through the middle of her. Russ couldn't stay behind. He just couldn't! He'd be killed.

The tram car lurched and began to move. Emma barely noticed it as she continued to shout at the glass, hoping Russ would change his mind.

Just look at us, she thought. *Look how much we need you. Don't do this. Please don't do this.*

But the car continued to move. It followed a gentle arc, riding the cables around a horseshoe cut in the floor. Then it swung out into the storm. A flurry of white surrounded them, and the wind nudged the suspended tram. As soon as Emma could no longer see Russ inside the station, her phobia took over.

The sorrowful void in her chest filled with hard-edged fear. Sweat broke out on her face and neck and palms. She felt the floor of the tram drop out, and suddenly the whole world was sideways and rushing up at her. A great crashing sound like waves on a beach thundered in her ears. She thought she might be sick. More than anything else, though, she felt the desperate need to be out of the tram, to be back on the ground. Her body trembled, and her mind screamed for her to escape this dangling coffin.

Emma closed her eyes and tried to breathe, though her tight chest made it difficult to draw air.

You're okay. Everything is okay. There's never been an accident on this tram. Never. It's fine. You'll be fine. . . .

But I won't be fine, her mind screamed back. *I won't. And I need to GET OUT OF THIS THING!*

Then Betina was beside her, wrapping an arm around Emma's shoulder. Emma had forgotten her friend, had forgotten Justin. When the panic took over, that was the only thing she could concentrate on. But she wasn't alone. She tried to ignore the fear and put on a brave face. Embarrassment added to her emotional disarray. She needed to chill and breathe and get through this.

She opened her eyes, intending to tell Betina that she was okay, but as soon as she saw the purple-gray atmosphere outside the tram car, the world fell sideways again. Emma bit down on her lower lip to keep from screaming.

Wind howled against the tram; the car swayed from side to side on the cable.

She squeezed her eyes closed tightly and shook her head furiously.

Get me out of here. Get me off this thing!

"Think about something else," Betina whispered. "Think about the beach. The hot sun. The warm sand."

"I-I've never been to the beach," Emma replied.

"Then think about a park. You've been to a park?"

"Y-yes."

"Okay, then picture a long field of grass. It's just been mowed, and the air is really sweet with the scent of it. You're under an oak tree. You're on your back looking up at the thick branches and all the leaves. Count the leaves. The sun is peeking through them and you imagine the leaves are fairy wings, their edges glowing with sunlight."

It was working. Emma didn't know if it was the soothing tone of Betina's voice or the image she'd placed in Emma's head, but the desperation was fading away. She pictured the emerald green field and remembered the smell of freshly mowed grass. It came to her with surprising clarity. The sky was clear, and the sun glowed like a yellow ball. She could almost feel its warmth on her face.

Then the tram rocked against a violent blast of wind and the image blew apart. Dread filled her mind like a torrent of ice water. Emma whimpered as the vertigo returned.

"Shh, it's okay," Betina said. "You're in a park. Lying down. Count the leaves."

Emma breathed deeply and reconstructed the fantasy as best she could.

"Justin and I are there," Betina said. "We're lying next to you, because it's a perfect day."

Russ should be here too, Emma thought. *He should be with us.*

Instead of Betina and Justin, Emma pictured Russ with her in the park. They lay on their backs, holding hands, staring up at the web of light outlining the leaves above.

He's so brave. He sacrificed himself so the rest of us could escape. Let him be okay. Don't let Tess get him.

Fear seeped into her thoughts. She forced herself to concentrate on the park, the tree, and Russ.

"Is she okay?" she heard Justin ask.

Betina didn't answer immediately. When she did, her voice was confident. "She's fine." Emma heard the lie in her friend's voice but tried to ignore it.

The tram ride seemed to be endless. Emma didn't know how long she stood there, eyes closed, holding a plastic handle in her tense fingers, but it struck her as a very long time. She felt the car ease up over the ridge and begin its descent. This wasn't as bad as the climb, but it was still frightening, and she kept trying to imagine herself in that park, on the firm ground with grass tickling her neck. Certainly they would be there any minute. It couldn't be that far.

"I see the resort," Betina told her. "It's all lit up, so we know they still have power."

"Good," Emma whispered in between deep breaths.

Before she knew it, the tram car came to a stop. It rocked back and forth, the wind still buffeting the sides.

Thank God, she thought, relieved to know she'd be out of the thing in a matter of seconds. She listened for the sound of the doors opening.

"Oh no," Justin said.

Emma cautiously opened her eyes and looked out in terror at the view through the tram car's window. Something was wrong. The resort stood a great distance away. She could see its lights, but they were far off. Snow lashed the tram in great sheets, creating a gray smear on either side of the dull yellow glow of the resort's lights.

The car had stopped, but they were still hanging in the air, high above the ground!

No, no, no, no, nononono.

30

Justin remembered his first ride on the tram. It had happened only six months ago, and he'd ridden over the ridge with his father, while his stepmother, Brandy, stayed home with his baby brother. His father, Jim, had managed the development of the Hawthorn Resort from Houston, but more opportunities in Winter, Colorado, had arisen, and the family had soon relocated. There had been eight other people in the car then, associates of his pops and a contractor brought in to complete the interiors of the hotel. Basically, Jim Moore ignored Justin, preferring to share gab with his buddies, corporate geeks who hung on his every word. Justin had looked out over the beautiful valley, amazed by the perfect little village, which had reminded him of the sort that often accompanied a model train set. The ridge itself was bare, just gray rock with bits of scrub brush emerging from nooks in the stone. As the tram car reached the top of the ridge, the resort land appeared. Snow covered the peak above and ran halfway down the mountain in white bands, showing where the ski runs had been made in the slope. The hotel's exterior was already complete and it stood like a tower over the smaller buildings that had once served the needs of skiers — equipment rental shops, a restaurant, a twenty-room lodge that now crouched in the shadow of the Hawthorn. As the tram car began its descent toward the hotel, Justin's father had spoken to him.

"This is what it's all about, champ," Jim Moore had said. "Take a nothing little town and make it something. Give them industry and a leg up into the twenty-first century. It just takes a little push. Some of those folks are grumbling now, but in a year, when their houses triple in value, they'll be thanking me. You wait and see."

One of his father's crews had blasted the mountain. They'd opened a cave and removed a box from a dark hole in the earth. What emerged from that box was nothing short of evil.

No one in Winter would be lining up to thank Jim Moore. More than likely, no one would be left.

The tram car swayed in the wind. That was all it had done for the last ten minutes, ever since its forward progress down the mountain had stopped. Justin looked ahead at the Hawthorn. Lights burned around the building's edges and poured from a number of windows. From this distance it looked as if it were carved from the snow, a solid, pale edifice amid a flurry of white. They had come so close to reaching it. Though he'd hated Russ's plan initially, once they were on the tram, Justin had warmed to the idea, if only because the worst was behind them. The village was decimated—the people crazy. But the madness was on the other side of the ridge now. Justin had seen the lights of the resort and his heart had swelled with relief. Now, the illumination burned through the heavy snowfall, teasing and infuriating.

"I don't believe this," he growled. "We're only three minutes away from the damn hotel."

"Something must have happened to Russ," Betina said for the fourth time. She was still holding Emma's shoulders. Ever since the car had stopped, Emma had been in bad shape, shaking and breathing deeply, trying to keep her fear in check.

"I know. But what are we going to do?" Justin asked.

"What *can* we do?" Betina replied. "There's no way to operate the system from the car. We've already pushed the emergency button, but it's not like anyone's around to hear an alarm."

Emma's head was down. Her eyes were closed. The storm beyond the glass made Justin think of snow globes.

Only this is different, he thought. *This is the reverse of a snow globe. Inside is clear and calm. Outside is the chaos of snowflakes and shifting currents.*

He rested his head against the glass door and looked down. The ground was obscured by the storm. How far down was it from the car? Twenty feet? A hundred? It was impossible to know, like trying to guess how deep an ocean was beneath a layer of fog.

But it's not impossible, he told himself. *You've been on this system half a dozen times.*

He tried to recall the layout of the ground and the distance between it and the car. He knew the drop-off was far steeper on the other side of the ridge, where the mountainside just sort of fell away beneath the cables and the car. On the resort side of the ridge the car was relatively close to the ground, or at least that was how he remembered it. With all of the snow that had accumulated, the drop might not be bad at all.

If you don't fall on a tree branch or a boulder.

"I have to get out of here," Emma said.

Her voice was remarkably calm, but Justin heard

the underlying panic. He couldn't imagine what she was going through.

"We'll be okay," Betina said. "If we have to, we'll ride it out up here. Tess can't reach us here. You just have to relax. Picture the park."

"I can't," Emma complained. "I *can't*. All I can think about is this thing crashing down and crushing me. Everything keeps turning over in my head. I feel the car turning over and falling. I feel it!"

Betina cast a worried look at Justin. He didn't know what to do, but he knew they had to do something. Emma was close to snapping.

"Help me get the doors open," Justin said. "There has to be a switch or a button somewhere."

"They aren't going to have a button just anyone can press to open the doors," Betina told him. "Some kid tries that and the place gets sued by a dozen scared passengers."

"Fine," Justin said. He cocked back his arm and swung the fireplace poker at the glass. It was thick. Reinforced. A small divot appeared on the pane at shoulder level.

He swung again.

"What are you doing?" Betina shouted.

"Emma can't stay in here, and we don't know what

happened to Russ. I do know that the tram rides pretty close to the ground on this side. The snow will cushion our fall."

"Are you insane? I'm not jumping into that." She pointed at the blizzard raging outside the car. "We have no idea what's down there, or how far down it is."

"I'll go first," Justin told her. He took another swing at the glass and a long crack ran diagonally across it. "If it's okay, I'll call back up to you."

"We won't hear you through the storm."

"You'll hear me," he said. He reared back and swung at the glass, finally shattering it. Shards fell into the blizzard, disappearing into the miasma below. A blast of icy wind struck him, and Justin stumbled back.

The car swung from the cable as the storm moved into the tram.

"Great!" Betina screamed over the wind. "Now if you jump down there and break your neck, we'll freeze to death."

Justin looked at the opening in the tram. Snow blew inside like confetti. He hadn't thought about the ramifications of smashing the window. Jumping out had struck him as the only plan—and now, it was.

How did things get so screwed up? he wondered.

Last night his biggest worry had been getting caught by his father for having a party. His notion of punishment had gone no further than a couple weeks of grounding or having his credit card confiscated. Now every decision was life and death.

"It'll be okay," he said nervously. He'd prove it was the right thing to do. All he had to do was jump and show them. He peered at the hole in the side of the tram. He walked up to the edge and looked. "We'll make it."

Then Justin stepped into the storm. For a moment he hung there and the snowflakes raced past him. Soon it seemed that the snowflakes' descent had slowed and even frozen for a second. Then they were moving in reverse, flying upward away from him.

Gravity pulled, yanking Justin through the dark haze. Down and down and down.

31

Emma opened her eyes in time to see Justin disappear into the night. One moment he stood in the door of the tram, and the next he was gone. Her heart leaped into her throat, and for the first time in what seemed like hours, her anxiety wasn't caused by the height and her confinement.

"Dumbass," Betina said, shaking her head.

"He had to do something," Emma whispered. "We couldn't stay up here forever."

"Well, he might have discussed it with us. He didn't have to just smash out the glass. What are we supposed to do if he doesn't make it? It's not like this thing had heat to begin with, but at least the wind and the snow were off of us. Now we're exposed. That's why they call it dying from exposure, you know?"

"He had to do something," Emma repeated. She eased away from Betina and walked toward the opening in the side of the car. Several feet away from the edge, she stopped. She hadn't meant to, but her legs froze as another wave of panic fell over her. She listened, hoping to hear Justin's voice amid the storm's chorus.

"He probably got skewered by a fallen tree limb," Betina muttered.

"Shh." Emma remembered seeing Clete slipping on a log, a sharp branch punching through his side like a sword blade. She prayed nothing like that had happened to Justin. That would be just too awful.

Still, he should have reached the ground by now. Should have been shouting for them if the drop hadn't caused major damage, yet all Emma heard was the blowing wind.

At this point, did it really matter if he called for them or not? Betina was right. If they stayed in the tram, they'd freeze to death by morning. Besides, Emma didn't want to stay in the tram. The way it swayed in the wind terrified her. The cables creaked and with each new sound, Emma felt certain she would soon be plummeting to the earth surrounded by crushing metal.

But if I jump, and something bad happens—if I get knocked out or killed—Tess will eventually get the box. She'll open it again and no one will be able to stop her because they don't know what's inside.

"What should . . ."

"Shh," Emma repeated. Just before Betina had begun to speak, she'd heard something, but her friend's words had eclipsed it.

She leaned forward, though she refused to step closer to the opening. The sound came again. It was Justin. He was calling her name.

"Emma." His voice was quickly carried away by the wind. It returned a second later. "Betina. It's cool."

"He made it," Emma announced excitedly.

"Okay," Betina said, crossing the car to her side, "but can *you* make it? Are you going to be able to walk through that door?"

"I don't know. Yes, I think so. I mean, I have to, right?"

"You're being rational right now, and that's good, but your fear isn't rational."

"You could push me."

"No, I couldn't. You might not fall right. You could tip and land on your head. You have to do this, and you have to keep your head on straight when you do. Now, can you do this?"

The cable above her creaked, and dread tore a path across her chest. Emma looked at her friend and then looked at the door. She wasn't going to be trapped in this thing. No way. No WAY!

Emma's mind went blank, and she dashed toward the opening in the side of the tram. She didn't pause before stepping out into the air. She didn't even scream when she began to plummet toward the ground. She squeezed her eyes tightly closed and felt the pull of gravity.

She hit the snow with a hard thwush and found herself buried up to her shoulders in a drift. Opening her eyes once the shock of her fall passed, she looked around for Justin but couldn't see him amid the flurry. Still, relief crashed over her like warm water. All of her tension washed away beneath it. Her muscles relaxed and her heart rate began to slow for the first time in over thirty minutes. She was out of the tram, on the ground. Safe.

She wriggled one arm free and then another. She tried to lift herself from the drift but sank back down. Three feet away, a dark object rocketed past her and hit the snow with another *thwush*.

Betina.

"Are you okay?" Emma asked.

"I think I've got an ice-wedgie, but I'll survive. Where's Justin?"

"I'm back here," he said.

Emma couldn't turn around because of the packed

snow, but she was glad to hear his voice. "Are you okay?" she asked.

"Yeah. Let's just dig ourselves out and get to the hotel."

The blizzard had returned during their time in the tram, and the plows hadn't been on this side of the ridge all day. Emma moved as well as she could in the hip-deep snow. Betina and Justin huddled around her, and the three walked like a single six-legged beast.

To her right, Emma could see a line of streetlights arcing down a long drive that joined up with the highway a mile from the hotel. The road from the village cut along the other side of the ridge on her left, but it had no lamps and was impossible to see with the tremendous accumulation of snow.

"How many people work in the hotel?" Betina asked. "I mean, what are we looking at if they aren't normal?"

"Only about ten," Emma said. "Basically, it's just the management, but they'll be okay." *They have to be*, she thought. *Mom is in there.*

"There's more than that," Justin said. "There may only be ten staff members, but crews were still working on the interior of the place. So it could be twenty or more total."

"Are you sure they're still here?" Emma asked.

"No, but they could be. Dad was in a hurry to get this place together for the big opening, so he brought in a ton of guys to finish it."

"So this may be no better than the village?" Betina asked.

"We'll see."

The massive glass doors of the hotel came into focus. They were framed in brass and looked inviting despite the scrim of foul weather. A long forest green awning jutted away from the building, and the letters HR were scrolled over the awning's face in a fancy script.

"Somebody had better have coffee on," Justin said.

"I'd be just as happy if no one was home," Betina said. Her teeth chattered with the cold and she pushed in close to Emma. Suddenly, she must have realized what she'd said because she quickly added, "I didn't mean that. I'm sure your mom is safe."

"It's okay. Let's just get inside and find a computer."

The doors of the Hawthorn Resort parted in a smooth *whoosh*, and Emma tensed. She expected crazy managers and construction workers to come charging at them across the great lobby of the hotel, but they entered into warmth and silence.

The lobby was a spectacle of marble and bleached wood, cream-colored lounges and sofas, and a massive front desk situated between two black marble pillars. A chandelier made of hundreds of tiny crystal rectangles dangled above the gleaming floor. At the far end of the lobby beyond a sweeping staircase with a crimson runner were the doors to the restaurant where Emma's mother worked. The lights were off. To the right of this were more glass doors leading into a small bar. On her immediate left was the seating area with its soft and pleasant-looking couches.

"They'll have computers in the offices behind the front desk, and there should be a business center." Justin looked around as if trying to find something. "I think the business center is up on the mezzanine."

"There are computers *on* the front desk," Betina said, and pointed.

"Those are an intranet," Justin said. "They don't connect outside of the hotel."

"Let's go," Emma said, setting off across the lobby.

In a few minutes, they'd have the answers they needed. They would find a computer in one of the offices and discover the legend of Pandora. She only hoped they were right: that everything that was happening was reflected in the mythology. More than anything, she was afraid that the story wouldn't tell them how to stop the spread of this terrible insanity. What if no cure had ever been found?

But they had to have found something, she reasoned. If this kind of madness had been unleashed thousands of years ago, people would never have survived it. Everyone would have been wiped out.

Unless it was a matter of degrees.

A puzzle came together in Emma's mind. Pieces fitted and clicked uncomfortably as she followed Justin around the front desk to a door set into the wall.

If this is about sins like greed, lust, and gluttony, then wouldn't this be the next step? Urges like that were naturally present in people thousands of years ago, but they might not have been as refined or as advanced as they are now. Sloth and greed and gluttony are already so extreme in the world, wouldn't it make sense that notching them up, even a little, would appear as madness?

She'd seen it at school: classmates freaking out because they couldn't afford the latest gadgets, people who collected tech toys like action figures creating personal electronic stores in their bedrooms. Like

Justin. Gluttony was the same. She'd seen a news report talking about national statistics for obesity; they were astounding. Every one of those sins—greed, sloth, wrath, envy, pride, gluttony, and lust—had been amplified over the years. They weren't even considered sins any longer. In fact, television commercials, magazine ads, and just about everyone she'd ever met made Emma think these were traits to be aspired to.

Then Tess opened the box and released those silver creatures, further enhancing behaviors that were already so strong.

Emma's head grew light as the realization overwhelmed her.

We were only a small step from insanity before any of this started.

"Door is locked," Justin said, still holding the knob in his hand. "There may be an employee entrance around the side of the building."

"I'd prefer to stay inside," Betina said.

"Then let's hit the mezzanine."

Betina turned to Emma and said, "Do you want to find your mom?"

No, was the first answer that came to her mind. She wanted her mother to be safe, wanted to see her, but

Emma was afraid she wouldn't find the woman who had spoken to her on the phone earlier that day but rather some crazy variation of that woman.

Where was everybody? Why weren't they gathered in the restaurant or the bar? The hotel looked spotless, but it felt wrong.

Besides, it could take a long time to find her mom. She might be in one of the rooms upstairs or hiding in the basement or something. Tess Ward would have a hard time getting to them at the hotel, but Emma didn't believe the girl had given up. They needed to find out exactly what was happening, and exactly how to stop it.

"We should get the information we need first," Emma told Betina. "And we need to reach someone outside of town to let them know what's happening. Once we do, I'll look for Mom."

"Are you sure?"

"Yeah. Ten minutes isn't going to make any difference."

They started climbing the staircase. Emma pulled the book bag off her aching shoulder and clutched it tightly to her chest.

A scream pealed out from deep in the hotel, reaching the lobby and spreading into an echo. Another cry followed: a different voice, lower and sounding more like a howl. Then Emma heard shoes slapping on tile, the stomping cacophony matching the fast rhythm of her startled heart.

32

No, Justin thought. *No more.*

He was tired of running, tired of freezing his ass off. A crowd raced down the corridor toward him. He could see their bustling and hear the noises they made, though he had yet to see one of their faces clearly. The madness had reached the Hawthorn Resort, and now he was trapped in the hotel with it.

"Upstairs," Betina said, already climbing.

But Emma remained, holding the book bag close to her chest, and so did Justin. He clutched the fireplace poker in a tight grip.

Too much running. Too much hiding. He wanted to go home and be warm and sleep for a week. All of this action-movie crap had to stop. They needed to get rid of the box and walk away and let Tess and the others tear themselves apart over it. He was done.

Seven people raced into the lobby of the hotel and Justin leaped off the stairs and tensed with the iron thrown back over his shoulder. But there was something different about this mob. They didn't have crazy eyes. Their faces weren't all messed up, sunken, and sick-looking. Three women and four men skidded to a halt when they saw him.

"He's one of them," a fat guy in a red sweater stated fearfully. He threw his arms out to hold back the rest of his group. "He's sick like the others."

Justin didn't immediately understand that they were talking about him. He was so confused, he looked over his shoulder at the lobby and the front desk, searching for whomever the fat guy was talking about.

"Mom," Emma said, from the staircase.

"Emma!" shouted a slender woman with full, dark hair. She tore away from the crowd, completely ignoring the protests of the rest of her party.

Emma's mom sped past Justin, who stood like a statue on the lobby floor. She ran up the stairs to greet her daughter, and the two embraced tightly.

"I didn't know what happened to you," Emma's mom said. Her words flowed out in a tearful torrent. "I tried calling every number I could think of, but all the phones are dead. I was so worried. God, I just . . . But you're okay? Are you okay?"

"I'm okay," Emma said. She sounded happy, though she was crying also. "I tried calling you too, but things have just been so crazy."

"What's going on?" a tall, slim guy with shiny black hair asked. "We haven't been able to get any word from the village in hours, and we've been trapped out here with a bunch of nutballs."

The crowd of adults all looked at Justin expectantly, as if he were suddenly in charge of everything. They wanted to know what was going on, and they expected him to know it. Emma and her mother continued with their joyful reunion, both talking a mile a minute. At the top of the stairs, Betina poked her head from around the corner and gazed out suspiciously over the lobby.

"The whole town is sick," Justin told them.

Faces falling, eyes clouding with concern, the adults pressed closer together as if they stood at the graveside of a friend.

"That's crazy," the fat guy in the red sweater said. "A whole town can't just lose it overnight."

"Tell that to the guy who almost put a screwdriver through your eye," the black-haired man replied.

"Well, I don't believe it."

"You heard what the state troopers said as well as we did. They were getting calls right up until the phones went out."

The two men continued to argue as the rest of the adults pulled away from them. On the stairs, Betina had joined Emma and her mother and the three spoke excitedly. Justin was so relieved to find other normal people that his shoulders went slack, and he realized he was still holding the fireplace iron in the air. He let his arm drop to the side and he relaxed for what felt like the first time in days.

"But we're still cut off," a beautiful blond woman only a few years older than Justin said. She wore a shape-hugging navy blue suit over a white blouse. A nameplate on her lapel read Alicia. "The state troopers are on the road, trying to get it cleared, but it's going to take hours. They said we could be here until morning."

"You've been in touch with the state police?" Betina addressed the crowd as she stepped down the staircase. "You can call them?"

"There's an emergency radio system in back," another woman said.

"Do you still have an internet connection?" Emma asked, suddenly turning away from her mother.

"Yeah," the fat guy replied. "All of the computers are up and running. We can get on the Web, but there's no news. Nobody from the village is online."

Justin remembered something the black-haired man had said. "There are other people up here?" he asked. "You said something about construction workers?"

The fat guy nodded. "They were up here finishing work on the lounge, the one on the mezzanine."

"How many?"

"I think there are five of them left," the man said. "They, uh, well, they killed the rest."

"Where are they now?"

"Locked up in the wine cellar," Emma's mom said. "They chased one of us down there, and we couldn't help her. We tried, I swear, but it was too late. We closed the door and locked it."

"And piled a bunch of boxes in front of the door," the fat guy added. "They aren't getting out."

"I need to use a computer," Emma said, "unless one of you knows anything about Greek mythology."

"I studied mythology in college," the blond woman, Alicia, said. Her face crinkled with curiosity as she looked at Emma.

"Why in the hell would we care about Greek mythology?" the black-haired man said. "If you haven't noticed, there's something of a crisis going on right now. Don't you think the homework could wait?"

"She knows what she's doing," Betina replied angrily.

"What do you know about Pandora's box?" Emma asked the blond woman. "Do you remember the myth?"

"Of course, it was one of my favorites."

"Tell me. I need to know everything you know about it."

"Why?" Emma's mother said. "Honey, what is all of this?"

"I just need to know!"

The other adults crossed the lobby until everyone stood at the foot of the stairs, like children gathering for a ghost story. Justin saw that. Alicia looked nervous. She was suddenly the center of attention, and it startled her, but her surprise passed quickly and she started to speak.

"Well, it started with Prometheus," Alicia began. "He angered the gods by giving the gift of fire to man. Now, there are several different tellings of this myth. Most of them are clearly based in misogyny, but what can you expect from such a male-dominated culture . . . ?"

"Please," Emma said, "can you just tell us what happens?"

"Okay. Sorry. When I say Prometheus was punished for giving fire to *man*, I mean just that. According to the mythology, women hadn't been created yet, but Zeus was so upset with Prometheus, he created Pandora, the first woman, and offered her as a gift to Epimetheus. That's Prometheus's brother. Finding her beautiful and charming, Epimetheus accepted Zeus's gift and Pandora entered the mortal realm. Pandora, which translates to something like 'all-gifted,' was deceitful and sent to cause mankind pain, but she was only part of man's punishment. When she entered our realm she brought a jar with her, a jar filled with unimaginable torments, diseases, and pains. Over the centuries, the myth evolved. Different cultures defined the contents of the jar according to their own belief systems, which is why one interpretation of the story suggests that sins were released. Of course, sin as we know it is a Judeo-Christian construct and not directly applicable to Greek myth."

"A jar?" Justin asked. "I thought it was a box."

"Depends on the translation and interpretation, but the popular thinking now is that Erasmus mistranslated the original poems that recounted the story. He took *pithos*, which means 'jar,' but translated it as *pyxis*, which means 'box.' That's become the popular version. In the end, it all refers back to woman as a vessel. A vessel of evil, if you want to be specific, which is why the story is so terribly misogynistic. In actuality, men have historically . . ."

"But how did they stop it?" Emma asked.

"Stop it?" Alicia asked.

"The evil," Emma insisted, "once it was released, how did they stop it?"

"Someone's here!" the black-haired man announced.

Justin turned in the direction the guy was looking. His arm was outstretched, pointing at the front doors across the lobby. They were lit up brightly, the space beyond them seeming to glow as high-powered lights burned against thousands of snowflakes.

"The state patrol made it," Emma's mom said. "Finally."

The adults muttered in relief. "Thank god." "It's about time." "Get me out of here." All of them, including Alicia, began moving toward the door. Justin was surprised when Emma grabbed Alicia's arm and tugged, pleading with her to continue.

"How does the story end?" Emma insisted.

"There are a number of different versions of the

story. They all end differently."

"Then tell me all of them. Tell me how to stop this!"

Alicia looked at Emma like she was insane. She pulled her arm away and moved on toward the front doors, which were already opening.

Justin's heart sank when he saw who was walking through the entrance. He hardly noticed the crowd of people behind her, bustling like fans at a pop star's back.

Tess Ward entered the Hawthorn Resort. Her shredded white coat settled around her narrow form as she entered the warm, still air of the hotel. A swarm of silver specks surrounded her head like a twinkling cloud.

Then her insane mob poured through the doors, dozens of them stampeding over the marble. Justin saw Kit Urban among them. His face was battered and cut. His eyes were white and wide. Drool spilled from the corners of his mouth in long, glimmering threads.

Screams rose up from the adults. From Betina. From Emma.

Justin spun away from the attacking mob. When he saw Emma on the stairs, cringing and clutching the book bag to her chest, he knew what he had to do.

He ran toward her. Fingers scrabbled for purchase on his back, but he was too fast for his attacker. When he reached Emma he didn't look at her, didn't even pause. He shot out his hand and grasped the book bag, which still held the box.

"What are you doing?" Emma cried, trying to back away.

"I'm saving my life," Justin said.

He looked at her then. Hurt and disappointment veiled her face. She shook her head slowly and yanked on the book bag. But Justin was stronger. He pulled, nearly sending Emma off her feet. When the bag came free in his hand, he spun, holding it high above his head.

"Wait!" he called to Tess, who remained by the hotel entrance. "The box is in here. Just take it and leave us alone. We won't cause any trouble."

"Justin," Emma shouted.

A disgusting grin spread over Tess's silvery face. "My beloved," she whispered amid the crackling static of the swarm.

"Yeah, right," Justin said. "Your beloved. Just take it."

"You can't do this," Emma said tearfully at his back.

"It's over, Emma," Justin said. "There's nothing else we can do."

"You're half right," Tess said, creeping forward across the hotel lobby. "There *is* nothing else you can do. But it's not over. Not for any of you."

"Hey," Justin called. "I'm giving you the box. Take it. Take whatever you want, just leave *me* alone."

"No," Tess said with amusement.

Tess's victims rushed forward, surrounding him. Justin shouted, trying to bargain with Tess, but the voices of the insane drowned him out.

It wasn't fair. He'd given her the damn box—he would have given it to Doug that afternoon, but Emma had gotten the stupid idea of running off with it. If it hadn't been for her, he'd be at home right now, warm and safe.

Faces smeared with blood and bits of food filled his vision. The book bag was torn from his grasp. Hands reached for him. In seconds he was encased in a tomb of foul-smelling, ragged clothes. Fists connected with his back and his head. The blows lacked force as his attackers couldn't take clear shots, but this was of little consolation. The fists kept hitting him, following him down as he slipped to the marble.

The bodies descended on him, covering him up, obscuring all light until he was in total darkness, as if the final shovelful of earth had been thrown on his grave.

33

There was buzzing. Everything was dark. Emma couldn't see, but that was because her eyes were closed. She tried to move, but she couldn't. The scent of flowery room freshener filled her nose. She didn't remember this scent from the lobby.

The screams had stopped. That was good. But there was buzzing, and there was pain.

The last thing she remembered was her mother screaming as a horde of terrible people surrounded her. Emma had raced forward, trying to help, but then the world had gone black.

Had someone hit her? Had she been unconscious? It would certainly explain the pain in her head.

The box! What had happened to it?

Emma opened her eyes.

She was sitting in an ivory-colored chair. Nylon cords wrapped like bracelets around her wrists, securing her to it. Her ankles were similarly bound.

She was in one of the rooms of the Hawthorn Resort. It was decorated in soothing shades of cream and ivory and beige, accented with forest greens and crimsons. At her back, she could feel cold air radiating from the window. The bed was on her left, the door straight ahead.

Her last moments with Justin, his betrayal, returned to her with crystal clarity. She hadn't believed what he was doing—after all they'd been through together. He'd all but tried to trade Emma and the others—not to mention the box—for his own freedom. She'd hoped it was a trick, a plan Justin had come up with at the last minute to keep the box from Tess and save their lives. But the only life he cared to save was his own.

Her disappointment with Justin turned to hot anger, burning through her. Russ had been right. He was just another selfish rich kid. Emma struggled with her bonds, using her newfound fury against the chair and the cords. She yanked and pushed with her arms, the cords scraping over her. Then a sound rose from her left, and Emma's struggles ceased.

She wasn't alone.

Someone was in the bathroom. Drawers opened and slammed. Frantic gasps, as if the person were suffocating, ripped through the room. A shadow appeared against the bathroom door, then vanished.

Emma's struggles against her bonds redoubled. She tried twisting her wrists, tried kicking her feet, but the cords held her firm.

A woman backed out of the bathroom. Emma could tell by the hair and the clothes that it was her mom, and her heart warmed.

She's okay, Emma thought. *Thank god.*

"Mom," she said. "Untie me. We have to stop her."

Her mom spun around and fixed a lunatic stare on Emma. Her cheeks were sunken. Deep lines appeared at her eyes and her mouth.

"So hungry," she whispered.

Emma's blood turned to ice. Her mom was sick; Tess had done it to her. That was the only reason Tess had let Emma live. Having the mob rip Emma apart would have been quick, and Tess wanted to be cruel.

It was pure spite. Emma had eluded Tess all day, had forced the girl to chase her across the village and over the ridge, keeping the precious box away from the freak. This was a unique punishment, a merciless penalty for defying Tess's command.

Emma's mom scurried to the door in a hunched and lurching gait, holding her stomach as if it ached. She tried the handle, yanked with all of her strength, and then let out a shriek. "Hungry!" she cried.

And there was nothing in the room to eat, Emma realized. She flashed on the memory of a woman crouched by the tram station—her bloody face buried in the carcass of a dog as she tore away its skin and chewed.

The gluttons will eat anything. They just need to eat and eat and . . .

Then the full extent of Tess's punishment came clear to Emma, and she screamed.

She was locked in the room with a lunatic who would soon come to see her as food.

Her mom threw back the closet door and crawled inside, searching the carpet for crumbs. It was irrational. The rooms hadn't even been used yet. No random bits of bread or wayward peanuts were going to be found there. Her mom was beyond desperate. How long before she gave up on the futile search and turned to her daughter for sustenance?

"So hungry," her mom shrieked, punching the wall at the back of the closet. She crumpled into a ball, curling up like an infant and clutching her stomach. "It hurts. It hurts so bad. I just need something. A little something. So hungry."

Emma fought against her bonds. Tears glazed her

eyes, making the scene before her smear. She blinked rapidly to clear her sight. She needed to keep an eye on the crazy woman in the closet. Her mom.

When her vision refocused, she saw that her mom was staring at her. The gaze was radiant, as if white fire burned behind the corneas.

"Just a taste," her mom whispered, licking her lips. "Just one little taste."

Emma screamed again. She didn't know what else to do. Maybe she should have been rational, tried to reason with her mother, but she was too scared.

Her mom uncoiled from her place on the closet floor and crawled on all fours across the carpet. Drool spilled over her lower lip, and she opened her mouth. When she reached the chair, her gaze ran frantically over Emma as if she were a buffet. Trembling hands reached out and clasped either side of Emma's head. Emma shook as hard as she could, but her mom's grip was too strong. Her mother's face, mouth open and slicked with spit, hovered only inches from Emma's.

"Just a taste," her mom said, leaning in and opening her mouth wider, revealing her perfect white teeth.

A pounding on the door shocked Emma out of her hysterical state. Her mom reared back, startled.

"Emma!" a boy's voice called. "Emma, are you in there?"

The pounding returned with greater force. Like thunder it rolled through the room.

"Help me!" Emma cried. "I'm in here. Help me!"

"The door's locked."

Emma's mom turned back to her. "So hungry."

"The kitchen," Emma said. Her voice cracked and shook as she spoke. "There's all the food in the world down in the kitchen. Open the door and you'll never feel hungry again."

Her mom's face screwed into an expression that was part suspicion, part hope. "All the food in the world?"

"Yes," Emma said through her tears. "Everything you could ever want."

The boy continued shouting at the door. He was kicking it now, but it wasn't going to budge.

"So hungry," her mom said.

Then the woman spun away and raced at the door. She flung it open and charged into the hall, knocking the boy into the far wall of the corridor. The door eased closed, and he recovered himself just in time to reach it before it latched shut.

Emma tried to see who had come to her rescue,

but the door obscured him. Then, he slowly pushed open the door and stood on the threshold, staring at Emma. He looked relieved to see her—worry fading from his eyes.

Russ. It was Russ!

Emma's heart welled. She was so glad to see him. Not only because he'd saved her life, but because he was okay. He was safe. She thought he'd been killed while protecting the tram station, but here he was. Bruises stained his face, and long cuts released tufts of padding from his jacket, but he was alive.

"I can't believe it's you," she said.

Russ crossed the room, trying to smile, but the expression fell too quickly. "I thought I was too late." He knelt beside her and began to untie the knots in the nylon cord. "The place looked empty when I got here. Then I found Betina, and she told me they'd taken you up to one of these rooms, but I didn't know if you were, you know, different."

"I'm fine, and you said Betina was okay?"

Russ shook his head. "I said Betina told me where you were. She's not exactly okay. She's crashed out on the floor. She doesn't look like she's hurt too bad, but . . ."

"What did Tess do to her?"

"She's like that woman in the house, except she's not quite that far gone yet. I could barely get her to talk to me, though. She kept saying some weird crap, like she's tripping or something."

Russ finished untying Emma's right hand and he ducked low to work on the bonds at her ankles.

"How did you know what room I was in?" Emma asked.

"I didn't." He finished untying her right ankle and moved around the front of the chair to concentrate on the left side. Emma flexed her hand and moved her foot to get the circulation moving in them. "Betina told me you were in one of the guest rooms, so I just took the elevator up, hoping something would clue me in."

"You heard me screaming?"

"Yeah, but not until after I found the room. They used this kind of cord to tie your door handle to one across the hall so the door couldn't be opened from the inside. I had to untie it. Now I guess I know why they wanted to lock you in. Who was that woman?"

"My mom," Emma said.

"Oh crap, are you kidding?"

"No."

"What was she doing?"

Emma couldn't bring herself to tell him. It was too sick, and she just didn't want to relive it.

"Sorry," Russ said, sensing he'd said something wrong.

When he finished untying her, Emma sprang to her feet and wrapped her arms around Russ's neck. She held him tightly. At first, Russ stiffened and backed away from the embrace, as if he were being attacked, but he gave in and returned the hug.

"So is that it?" Russ asked, once Emma pulled away. "Did we lose? Are we totally screwed or what?"

"Maybe," Emma admitted. "I don't know. Let's get to a computer and find out."

Emma stared at the monitor in disbelief, reading over the same paragraph again and again. Nausea crept up her throat and lodged like a rock on the back of her tongue.

We were so stupid, she thought. *So stupid. We had the box this whole time, and . . .*

"What does it say?" Russ asked. "Does it say anything about how to stop this?"

"Sort of."

"Well, what do we have to do?"

"We have to open the box. *Again.*"

"Do *what*?"

"According to the mythology, when the box was opened, all of this badness escaped—the sins, evil, whatever you want to call it. But the vessel was closed before everything got out. Hope was trapped inside."

"I don't follow. What good is hope going to do us?"

"It's all a metaphor," Emma said. "It's a myth. They change a lot of stuff. The Greek gods didn't create Pandora or this box, it was a story to explain what happened when someone found that thing, or something like it, and released what was inside. Back then, the influence of those silver insects might have pushed some people to the edge, but we're already so far gone, we're just falling over it. So maybe opening the box a second time will release something that snaps people out of it. A cure. Something."

"But you don't know?"

"No. Opening it a second time could just make things worse."

"I don't think things could get any worse."

"Never say that," Emma warned. "I'm just so pissed off with myself for not having done anything when we had the box. Tess has it now. I don't see how we'll ever get it back."

"You're sure she has it?" Russ asked.

"Yes," Emma said sadly. "Justin gave it to her."

"He *what*?" Russ's face turned red with anger. "I knew we couldn't trust him."

"There's nothing we can do about it now. It's gone. I feel so stupid. Tess didn't want the box so that she could open it again. She wanted it to make sure no one *else* opened it."

"Well, don't blame yourself. How could you know what would happen? Hell, if you open a door and see a room full of snakes, you're not going to open the door again to see if they might be friendly. You didn't know."

"And now I do, and it's too late."

"Maybe not," Russ countered. "She's trapped up here like the rest of us."

"And surrounded by a hundred crazies. We'll never get anywhere near her."

"So what do you want to do?"

Emma didn't know how to respond.

34

Russ fumed. He wanted to get his hands on Justin Moore and break the selfish little prick's neck. Emma refused to say anything more about how it had happened, but she didn't need to. Russ knew the rich boy had betrayed them, trying to save his own skin.

As they walked down the stairs from the mezzanine to the lobby, Russ told Emma how he'd managed to get to the hotel. It had been a close call at the tram station. A few of the crazies had fallen through the stairs, but most got to the door and through it. Russ had fought with them for as long as he could but finally realized he was dead meat if he didn't bail.

He'd leaped through the opening in the building where the tram cars came in on cables. The snow was deep and cushioned his fall. As he fled across the street to escape, he saw that Tess was already heading toward the ridge, riding shotgun in the snowplow that was clearing the street ahead. A horde of lunatic townspeople had followed her path.

"I figured you guys would be stuck on the tram," he

told Emma. "I mean, I didn't see the other car come into the bay, so I knew you hadn't made it to the station on this side yet. Earlier, Kit and I borrowed a snowmobile and ditched it when a bunch of those freaks came after us. After seeing Tess headed this way, I snagged the thing and started after her, but I had to stay way back because I didn't want her army to hear me coming. By the time I got here, the place was quiet."

"Betina!" Emma said, breaking into a run.

Russ followed Emma with his eyes and saw Betina lying on one of the cream-colored sofas across the hotel lobby. Her knees were curled to her chest, and her eyes were closed. She looked remarkably serene considering the day and night she'd had.

"She must have climbed up there from the floor," Russ noted. "I guess it's more comfortable."

Emma left Russ's side and ran across the lobby to her friend. She knelt down and touched Betina's head.

"It wants out," Betina said quietly. Her voice carried across the room to Russ.

"What do you mean?" Emma asked.

"Tired now." Betina closed her eyes and hugged herself tightly, nestling into the soft fabric of the couch. "This is nice."

"I guess it could have been worse," Russ said. "She could have turned brutal."

"Or hungry," Emma added.

"It wants out," Betina whispered into the cushion.

"That's what I'm talking about," Russ said. "She kept saying that when I was trying to find out where you were."

"I don't know what it means," Emma said. "If she's talking about what was in the box, it already got out."

No kidding, Russ thought. There had to have been a hundred people following Tess over the ridge. Maybe more.

"Wait a minute," he said.

A hundred people had come over the ridge, but where were they? They hadn't gone back to the village. He would have seen them. They would have blocked his path to the hotel, so if they hadn't returned to the village, where had they gone? A snowplow? A hundred people? Where *could* they go?

The other road, he thought. *The highway!*

"Tess is trying to escape," he said. "She wants to get out of town. That's what Betina's talking about."

"It wants out," Emma murmured, hating the way the words felt on her tongue.

"And if she gets out, she's going to spread that sickness. More cities are going to end up like Winter. Tess can go wherever she wants, all over the world. Do you have any idea what that could mean? Everything we know could be wiped out in a few months. Civilization over. The whole damn thing could end."

Emma looked terrified. Russ hated seeing the expression, but he couldn't do anything about that. He was right. He *knew* he was right.

"We can't let that happen," Russ said.

"We have to stop her," Emma agreed.

The snow fell and swirled. It filled the air, thicker than any fog bank Russ had ever seen. The snow-mobile drove through it, hardly disturbing the mael-strom of white.

They followed the rut in the snow left along the road by the snowplow. It was the only way they knew which direction to travel. Darkness and blizzard made it impossible to see far, so Russ drove slowly, keeping his eyes on the path. The hotel was far behind them; Betina remained on the couch, snuggling in tight to the expensive fabric. Russ envied her.

The weather continued to brutalize him and

Emma as they traveled over the uneven track on the snowmobile. Russ had to wipe at his face frequently because flakes accumulated on his lashes and ice-burned his eyes.

The only comfort was the feeling of Emma's arms around his waist and her chin on his back.

They had no plan, and that worried him, but they couldn't formulate a plan before they saw exactly what they were up against. He didn't even know if Tess would remain with the mob out ·in the storm or if she'd take refuge until her servants finished their work.

About that work, he was more certain. They were clearing the road, digging the highway out so Tess could escape Winter.

They had to be close, he reasoned. He and Emma had been riding for a long time, and even though they moved slowly, they couldn't have been far from the highway.

He nearly ran into a wall of snow before he noticed that the snowplow's path veered to the left. Then they were traveling upward at a steep angle.

The highway's on-ramp.

At the top, he stopped the snowmobile and killed the engine.

"They'll hear us coming," he shouted, to be heard over the storm.

"I know," Emma replied, already climbing off the machine behind him. "We'll have to walk."

They didn't have to walk far, though. Around the first curve in the road an amber glow radiated in the wall of white ahead. As they drew closer, Russ saw dark shapes moving and the outline of the plow refined. He led Emma to the shoulder of the road and pressed up against the rock of the mountainside.

"This is it," Russ said.

Before he knew what was happening, Emma's arms were around his neck and she was kissing him. He was so startled, he'd first taken her affection for an attack and backed right into a jagged rock. When her lips met his, warm and tender, he relaxed and wrapped his arms around her, pulling her as tightly as he could, not wanting her to slip away. For a moment, his fear melted.

Then Emma was pulling away.

Don't, he thought.

He gazed into her eyes and was saddened to see the worry there. It was unavoidable, he knew, but he wanted to keep the nightmare at bay. Emma wouldn't let him. The moment was gone.

"For luck?" he asked.

"Because I might not get another chance," she told him.

The memory of her lips still tingled on his, still warmed him. But he understood it was time to finish this thing and he nodded. He looked back at the mob, and at the plow idling in the fog of snow.

"How are we going to find Tess in this?" he asked. "We can't exactly walk around asking. They're going to tear us apart, so we need to find her, get the box, and get away fast."

"We aren't going to get away," Emma told him. "No matter what happens, if we go in there we'll never get back out unless we find that box and open it. Then we have to pray it works."

He knew she was right, and a numbing resolve filled him. It was the same determination he'd felt at the tram station when he'd closed the car door and sent it on its way, watching Emma and her friends fade into the night. He knew there was no way to control the entire world. It would carry on, sane or not, regardless of his needs and wants. His father and best friend were gone—alive or dead, they were different, terrible people now. His hometown was destroyed— broken and burned. Nearly everything he cared about had been taken away, changed, and destroyed.

Kit had always said that Russ wouldn't fight for anything, that he just accepted things and let them push him through life like wind in a sail. His father had always told him that he couldn't change the world. Maybe that was true, but only an idiot or a selfish fool wouldn't try. Russ knew the choice he had to make. He could lie down and surrender, or he could fight.

Russ wasn't going to lie down.

35

Emma eased into the mob, staying close to the mountainside. The faces that appeared around her were uniformly grotesque: bloody and bruised and sunken, with wide, startled eyes that never seemed to blink. The faces emerged from the swirling snow and vanished just as quickly, like ghosts passing through a spectral rift. They paid her no attention. They were intent on the work at hand. With their bare hands they hauled away chunks of ice and snow and rock. They scurried like insects over the mound covering the road. One man skidded on top of the heap. He fell on his face and slid down the bank, disappearing over the highway's edge. He didn't even scream.

The snowplow was idling in the middle of the road. Emma got as close as she could to it, checking to see if Tess Ward occupied one of its seats, but the girl wasn't to be found in there. Emma was disappointed. It would have made things easier if Tess were someplace obvious. Emma continued into the throng, reached the wall of snow that blocked the road, and grabbed up an armful so as not to draw attention.

Russ would arrive soon. She'd told him to give her five minutes alone in the crowd so she could find Tess.

Emma crossed the road, following the path of a dozen lunatics, and dumped her armload of snow over the edge. She watched the clump of dirty white vanish into the swirling flurry and backed away from the guardrail. She collided with someone and was shoved aside. Emma turned, and everything stopped.

Justin stood in the road. She barely recognized his face. His left cheek was swollen so bad, it looked like he had a lemon shoved in his mouth. Deep scratches ran in trails over his forehead and jaw. His neck was bruised, purple and black in places. One eye was swollen shut. The other eye glared out at her, filled with hate. He slapped the fireplace iron on a palm, like a policeman absently bouncing his nightstick.

"Justin," Emma whispered when her breath returned.

He didn't reply. Instead, he pulled the poker back and delivered a painful blow to Emma's thigh. Her leg crumpled beneath her and she cried out, tumbling to the hard-packed snow on the road. She rolled and tried to get to her feet, but Justin kicked her. His foot clipped her shoulder, sending her sprawling. She cried out and scrambled back as best she could. Other crazies were gathering now. She felt them pressing in on all sides of her. Legs like a forest surrounded her, but she couldn't take her eyes off Justin. He was monstrous, a vision of hate against the ferocious backdrop of blizzard.

Then Justin was gone, moved aside like a door to reveal something even more terrible.

Tess, or what had once been Tess, slid into Emma's view. Her shredded coat whipped in the wind. The silver creatures covered her in sliding, writhing sheets. Bands of them rose from her brow and swept back like a dreadful veil, trailing out in the wind. There seemed nothing human left of Tess, except the general shape of her. She looked mechanical, unnatural, and deadly.

"So persistent," Tess said. The wet rumble of her voice carried easily through the storm.

Emma noticed she wasn't carrying the box, and her heart sank further. This was it. Even if Russ arrived now, they were finished. Emma had expected Tess to be holding the box, protecting it, but she'd hidden it or entrusted it to one of her servants for safekeeping. Emma knew she and Russ would never survive long enough to find it now.

"We are impressed," Tess continued. "We thought you a mere annoyance, but you've shown us such admirable tenacity." Tess threw back her head in a pantomime of a laugh, though no sound issued from her gaping mouth. Tremors ran over Tess's body. The silver creatures moved in waves like loose skin. Something appeared for a moment on her exposed chest, but was quickly hidden when the silver things settled. "There is always a fight," Tess went on. "*Always*. At every turn, you fight, thinking you benefit from repression and willpower, but that is an unnatural state. You fight us because you prefer to fight with yourself. *Oh, mustn't do this. Oh, can't have that. Oh, how very bad I am to want all of the pretty shiny things.*"

"It's called being human," Emma shouted.

"It's pathetic."

"What are you?"

"We are a gift from elsewhere," Tess said. "We exist in many places, in many forms. We collect your urges, soak them up like a sponge, so you can go about pretending how very good you are. It sickens us. The taste of your need is foul, and it has fed us for centuries. We are full on it, gagging on the quantity of your wants.

So we give them back to you. Once you are gone, we'll never need to taste of it again."

"I don't understand," Emma said.

"Your kind never does." Tess stepped forward. "But it will all make sense once you experience it."

A silver speck lifted from Tess Ward's face. It lit in the air and circled for a moment before diving at Emma. She covered her face against the tiny attacker, but her effort was futile. She felt a hot point on her cheek, like the tip of a heated needle poking the skin. Emma scrubbed at the place with her hand, but the searing sensation traced up her cheek toward her eye. For a split second she saw it shimmer, hovering above the tear duct. Then it disappeared and the burning dot was in her head, sliding around her eyeball and working back to her brain.

No, screamed through her mind. *No. Not me. Not like Justin. Not like Mom. Please. Not me.*

A great roar erupted in her ears, and Emma thought the silver creature had already gone to work on her. But shouting soon followed. She raised herself against the snow padding the guardrail and watched in wonder as the crowd before her scattered and tumbled like bowling pins.

Russ revved the snowmobile's engine and continued

through the crowd, knocking people away left and right.

It's too late, Emma thought. *He got here too late.*

Tess Ward spun as Russ passed. The silver shroud covering her rustled and whipped at the air. Farther down the road, a crowd of people yanked Russ from the snowmobile and threw him to the ground. The sound of his impact was eaten by the wind. When Tess completed her spin, she had made a full circle. Emma again saw the strange object on Tess's chest and realized what it was:

The box.

It wasn't *on* Tess's chest; it was *in* it. Tess was gone. The silver creatures had devoured her but had maintained her shape as they worked their evil through the city.

Emma got to her feet and leaped forward. Still off balance, Tess tried to rear back, away from Emma's grasping hands. But her form was unstable.

Emma plunged her hands through the silver membrane and grabbed the box. She yanked with all of her force and fell back into the snow. Quickly her fingers worked over the front of the box. She pried at the lid, trying to get it open, but her fingers kept slipping off.

A horrible scream poured from Tess's throat, and

she lunged at Emma, silver-sharp nails aiming for her face. Emma threw up her hands, trying to deflect the attack with the box. It slipped in her hands, and she fought to keep hold of it. As she struggled, a sharp pain bit into her thumb. She'd cut herself on the thorn of the latch.

And the lid of the box flew open.

Emma saw a flash of golden light; it deepened to a thick bronze, obliterating her view of Tess and the snow and everything else. Droning filled her ears, like she'd stuck her head in a hive of bees. It confused her. But suddenly her fear was gone, and she was warm, so very warm.

36

The hands that had been tearing at his clothes pulled away. The feet stopped kicking him. The crowd that had been beating the hell out of him retreated. They shouted and screamed. They ran as if suddenly something more terrible than themselves had run into the road.

Russ tried to sit up, but he was too sore. Ahead of him was the wall of snow that had fallen across the road, bathed in the lights from the plow. The snowmobile sat broken, tipping. Its nose was buried in the accumulation. A dozen people stood on the bank above, jumping around and yelling frantically, pointing up the road. Russ rolled over onto his stomach to see what had their attention. Sharp pains shot up his leg, from ankle to thigh.

"Oh, man," he gasped, once his eyes settled on the scene before him.

Amid the roiling flakes of snow, another storm raged. A wave of radiant golden specks was rising. The wave's upper edge was ragged and narrowed into long, whipping points like flames, arcing over Tess Ward's head. But it wasn't really Tess anymore. The silver fragments that had formed her body were now loose and changing their form. At the center was still the torso of a girl, but the arms and the legs had grown thin. Soon they looked more like the tentacles of a sea creature than the limbs of a human. Then the body lengthened. The hair whipped upward, cresting like the golden wave facing her. The tattered white coat dropped to the ground, another lump among many in the road. In the snow lay Emma, limp beneath the golden wave.

The two metallic fields collided in the air. They wove tightly, gold and silver specks whirling frantically as if two swarms had declared war. The air crackled and snapped with static. The snow that fell into this struggle melted instantly, giving the scene an odd clarity. Narrow filaments, woven of the two elements, whipped away from the battle. More and more threads tore loose from the central mass. Soon, the core of the fight was gone, and the road and the plow and the remaining mob were covered in a mesh of glittering strands. Men and women slapped at the air, screaming at the top of their lungs. Others collapsed on the road as the net of dueling particles ensnared them.

Then, in a flash, the gold and silver strands were gone.

The road was silent.

And the snow kept falling.

Russ dragged himself over the packed snow toward Emma. She remained motionless, propped against the bank of snow at the guardrail. Next to her, the box lay on its side. The lid was closed.

Pain sang throughout Russ's body, but he needed to know that Emma was okay. He crawled on his belly, trying to ignore the agony and the cold until he reached her.

Her eyes sprang open the moment his hand touched hers.

"Are you okay?" he asked.

"Mmmm," Emma said, weakly nodding her head.

He pushed himself forward and managed to turn around so he too was propped against the banked snow, his shoulder touching Emma's. On the road, the mob looked around in confusion. One old man knelt behind the snowplow, weeping hysterically. Others cried too. Most were dumbstruck and staggered about like zombies, unsure of what to do or where to go next.

"Are they going to kill us now?" Russ asked.

"I don't think so," Emma replied. He noticed something different about her voice. It was weak but somehow very clear at the same time. "I think it's gone from them."

"So it's done?"

"No," Emma said. "Not quite. Those in the village are still stricken."

He rolled his head to the side to look at her. "What are we supposed to do?"

Emma turned to face him. A golden particle leaped onto her lip and crawled up her cheek like a tear defying gravity. More and more of them appeared at her mouth, spilling over onto her chin. "We know what to do," she said.

37

The spring thaw came late to Winter that year. It seemed the cold had latched onto the mountain and refused to let go. But one morning Emma woke and the sun was shining. She dressed and stepped outside and realized the bitter edge to the wind was gone. She stood on her front stoop with her face lifted upward, allowing the warm rays to wash over her. After many minutes she lowered her face and looked across the street at the other houses, and a twinge of sadness pinched her heart.

So many of them were still empty.

Inside, she made a go-cup full of hot green tea and slid on her jacket. At her closet she lifted a package off the shelf and tucked it under her arm. Then she left the duplex and began to walk.

On that terrible night, she had walked. After Tess Ward vanished amid a twinkle of metallic specks, after her followers fell into a daze, Emma had left Russ on the side of the road, knowing he was safe, and she'd started walking back down the highway to the service road and to the hotel. She'd found Betina on the couch in the lobby, met her mother in the kitchen and half a dozen men locked in the wine cellar. Insane when she'd arrived, they were little more than confused when she left. Her path took her back over the ridge into the village. She'd walked and walked and walked, meeting dozens, then hundreds of people. Night became morning and the blizzard was memory, but still she'd walked, guided by a quiet voice in her head that led her to those in need.

Once this trek was complete early the following afternoon, Emma collapsed. She woke up in the school gym a day later. The gym had been transformed into a makeshift hospital, handling the overflow of patients from the Winter Clinic. Her mother was there. Russ was in a bed two rows over, and he asked to be moved so he could be closer to Emma. They talked a lot. Held each other's hands. He asked if it was really over.

Emma told him it was, but that wasn't exactly true.

Today, she walked from her home and into the village. Construction crews were busy rebuilding the fallen structures on Main Street. This early in the morning, men and women in jeans and hardhats wandered the sidewalks, fresh cups of coffee in hand, reporting for the morning's work. Two of the Promenade stores had reopened, though business was slow. A tram car emerged from the back and began its slow climb up the ridge. Sipping her tea, Emma noted the progress the crews were making, and it warmed her to see it.

So many people were gone now; the town could have collapsed. But by small degrees it was coming back. A lot of people had moved immediately following that cold and terrible night, but those who remained were determined to rebuild.

She shifted the package from under her arm and held it against her chest before taking another sip of tea. The parcel wasn't heavy, but her shoulder had started to complain from the way she was holding it.

At the tram station, she waited with two other people. She knew them, had seen them at the Hawthorn Resort just before Tess had arrived that night. They were managers at the hotel. They nodded at Emma but didn't speak to her.

The Hawthorn had been left relatively undamaged, but of course its grand opening had been postponed. The new owners had opened for business a month ago, off-season. Her mom said business was picking up, but Emma could tell by the worry in her eyes it wasn't picking up fast enough.

It will be okay, Emma thought. She was certain of it.

"Good morning, Emma," Russ's dad said from his place behind the tram controls. His eyes twinkled and he wore a warm smile.

"Morning, Mr. Foster."

"Heading over to see your mom?"

"Yes," she said, even though she wasn't.

"Is that a present for her?" He nodded toward the package in her hand.

"No," Emma replied, "this is something else."

"Well, we're expecting you for dinner Friday."

"I can't wait," Emma replied. "Let me know what I should bring."

"Just yourself."

She continued to chat with Red Foster until the tram arrived. She climbed in and waved good-bye as the doors slid closed. Even though the ride no longer frightened her, she still closed her eyes and thought about a park, a tree, and Russ. When she opened her eyes, she was high above the ridge. The sky was a crystal blue above her. Below, the snow-covered ridge dropped off into the valley toward the village.

The authorities were confounded by that night in

Winter. So many people were hurt. So many were dead. But the perpetrators had outnumbered the victims, and many of the perpetrators were victims themselves. All kinds of scientists and law enforcement officials had descended on the town once the weather had cleared. None of them knew what to make of the situation. The reporters who had shown up in droves created a number of interesting stories, none of which came anywhere near the truth. They didn't seem to care, though. The ratings were high; they were happy.

In the end, very few charges were filed. The teams of scientists remained, testing the water and the soil and the bodies of some of the victims, looking for a toxicological explanation. The reporters had lost some of their interest; stories still appeared in the news, but most people in town had given up talking to the press.

The tram car peaked over the ridge, and Emma turned away to look at the striking tower of the Hawthorn Resort.

Justin's father had sold his interest in the hotel — and all of his other local property holdings — in the months following the blizzard. Even before his business dealings were settled, he moved the family away. Justin had not returned to school and was rarely allowed to leave the house. In the weeks before he moved, Emma had seen him only once. He couldn't even look at her. He lived in Connecticut now.

Once the tram was docked at the station beside the resort, Emma looked up the mountainside on her left. It was still thickly frosted with snow. The climb wouldn't be easy, but she had to make it.

It was her final obligation to the box.

She started walking, across the front of the hotel and toward a narrow path snaking up through the trees beside a white ribbon of ski run.

Of the people she'd known before the terrible night, Betina was the only one who didn't seem fazed by it. For her it was an interesting story to tell: *Remember when we slid down that hill into the snowdrift? Remember jumping out of the tram?* Her friend looked back on the night like it had been a series of extreme-sporting events. Betina, smart as she was, aware as she was, lived in complete denial. But Betina was still the best friend Emma'd ever had.

A branch snagged on her coat and Emma stopped. She shifted the package in her hand and balanced her cup of tea. Once free of the limb, she continued to climb.

Russ was another story. The night haunted him.

When he talked about it, which was infrequently, he did so with the utmost gravity. Most of the time he didn't want to talk about it at all, and that was fine with Emma. She was happy enough just being with him, going to a movie or sitting in front of a fire.

It took her two hours to reach the summit. When she emerged onto the plateau she saw the cave. Just big enough for a man to walk through without stooping, the cave's entrance had a manufactured appearance. Its rounded edges curved down in uniform arcs. Emma knew it wasn't man-made, but it looked that way.

That morning, feeling the sun on her cheeks, she'd known that today was the day she had to return the box. It couldn't be destroyed, and it couldn't be trusted in anyone's hands, not even hers. It had to go back into the earth.

One day it would be discovered again. Maybe not in her generation, or the next, but one day. It was a part of the nature of things, a fragment of life.

Emma looked out over the vista spreading down and away from the mountaintop. The crystal blue sky, the forest of pine, the veins of rock running through sheets of whitest snow. Far away she saw the village and beyond that, the foothills and beyond that, the whole rest of the world.

From so high up and so far away, it looked beautiful and unspoiled.

Many things were like that, if you didn't look too closely.

Tod hadn't seen the demon in years. . . .

He'd convinced himself that Blake was nothing more than a dream, a fantastical creature he and his friends Rachel, Veronica, and Simone had created to explain away the terrible thing that had happened.

Tod scrambled up the slope. Dirt slid away beneath his shoes, his knees, and his hands. His palm slapped down on a rock, and he grasped it tightly to steady himself. He hauled himself up over the edge.

Blake was already there, waiting.

Tod tried to scream, but the world around him went black before he could utter a sound.

Now Rachel, Veronica, and Simone must find a way to stop the evil being that has returned to haunt them—or die trying.